MW00682143

Hearts Remember

With a silent moan her hands began to stroke the smooth muscles of his chest and felt his gasp of breath as her fingers trailed over his belly.

Alex's voice reverberated in her ears. "Isabel. Isabel, we've got to stop."

Confusion wrinkled her brow until his meaning became clear. She looked deep into his heavy lidded blue eyes. "I don't want you to stop." Her voice low and throaty.

"But Isabel," Alex began but Isabel interrupted him.

"I love you, Alex." Isabel watched the creases in his forehead even out as he smiled.

"I love you too, Isabel, but are you sure you're ready for this? I mean, I don't know if—"

"I'm sure, Alex. I'm more sure of this than anything else in my life right now." Isabel ran her fingers through his damp hair.

Hearts Remember

By M. Louise Quezada

Genesis Press, Inc.
315 Third Avenue North
Columbus, MS 39701

Hearts Remember

ISBN: 1-885478-38-0

Manufactured in the United States of America

First Edition

Dedication

To Stewart, whose loyal love and support sustain me.

To Colton and Savannah, whose curious and adventurous spirit enliven me.

To Mom and Dad, whose never-ending source of love and encouragement fulfill me.

And no Nina Mary, whose courage and kindness inspire me.

Con mucho amor y gracias a todos!

Prologue

Denver, Colorado   August 1998

The party proved to be the diversion she needed. The anxiety from Ray's petulant call earlier diminished as she enjoyed the friendly atmosphere. Isabel
searched the room for Tony, whose tall lanky build and
Jimmy Smits looks always made him stand out in a
crowd.

From the corner of the room he motioned for her
to join him. "Ted Roberts, this is my good friend Isabel
Medina." Extending her hand, Isabel noted the smiling
eyes of the party's host.

"So you're the artist who painted those lovely
pictures in Tony's restaurant. Hope we can talk you into
donating a couple for the new one."

"I'd be happy to." Isabel's eyes sparkled at his
flattering comment. An instinctive feeling told her that
he and Tony would make great partners. "You don't
sound like you're from here," Isabel said, noting an
accent.

"No, Arlene and I were born and raised in

Austin, Texas," Ted answered. "Been in Colorado about three years and just love it but Texas will always be home."

For a brief second Isabel forced herself to keep focused on their conversation. Afterwards she admonished herself for letting things like that remind her of Alex. She had put the past to rest and that's where it would stay.

🏵 🏵 🏵

Lena Gomez watched as Isabel mingled with all the guests. *Who does she think she is, with her fancy red pantsuit and her hair piled on top of her head like she was some queen? While I'm working my ass off to please these undeserving snobs?* Well, tonight would be the last time. She'd paid her price.

Only an hour longer and this whole charade would be over. A perfect arrangement, after seeing the address posted on Tony's peg board, she begged him to let her work the party. Planning a rendezvous here and throw them off track.

Before hoisting her tray she patted the disc in her pocket. Her ticket to freedom.

🏵 🏵 🏵

Just after eleven o'clock Isabel silently slipped away and wandered out to the patio. She turned to see Lena Gomez exit the back door and walk around the side of the house. On a couple of occasions Isabel noted Lena's unfriendly attitude aimed solely at her but kept it to herself. If she did a good job for Tony then that's all that mattered.

Moments later Tony found her. "We can leave shortly. Eric will finish up for me. But Lena disappeared and I need her to help clean up."

"I saw her go that way a few minutes ago." Isabel pointed in the direction Lena had gone.

"Great. What the hell does she think this is?" Tony rose to go but noticed some late guests arriving. "Let me check and see if these people need anything. I'll meet you back here."

Isabel walked over to the corner of the patio where water softly trickled down a staircase of uneven rocks tucked into a garden. From the doorway, one of the late guests strained to see her profile in the moonlight.

A slight rush of air raised goose bumps on her arms. Isabel turned towards the house at the sound of Tony's voice. Joining him, they proceeded down the steps.

Isabel's eyes widened at the sight of Ray Calhoun standing with Lena near her open car door.

Isabel and Tony shared a look of puzzlement as they approached the twosome.

"Ray?" Isabel's breath caught in her throat. Under the street lamp's illumination she saw Ray's hand holding a gun. "What...What's going on?" she asked, trying to squelch the panic slicing through her.

A twisted smile greeted them both. Tony's arm shot out as he pushed Isabel behind him. "Ray, come on. Put the gun down," Tony pleaded.

"Just stay where you are." Ray turned his attention back to Lena. "Hand it over now."

"The money," Lena argued.

Ray passed Lena an envelope in exchange for a computer disc she handed him. "You'll get the rest when it's cleared."

"Ray. This is insane." Isabel's voice shook.

Ray spoke deliberately slow. "It's business, Isabel."

"Isabel? Isabel Medina?" A man's voice called out. Isabel rotated around, stepping from behind Tony. She saw the look of shock in the stranger's handsome face when he grasped their situation.

Ray reacted hastily, roughly pulling Isabel back against himself. Isabel's body stiffened as she held her breath. Cold hard steel pushed into her cheek. Her mind raced frantically. The stranger's identity registering. In the dim light piercing blue eyes touched her very soul. The chiseled jawbone clenched like she remembered. A raging sense of confusion filled her head. Panic, intermingled along with the emotions she buried so long ago now, wreaked havoc on any remaining thread of sanity.

Ray's deep voice penetrated her trance-like thoughts. "Just do as I say and nobody will get hurt," Ray ordered. "And you, buddy," Ray motioned to the newcomer, "you stay right where you are. Isabel comes with me."

Isabel's stomach churned as she felt his hot breath against her cheek. "I'll be okay Tony, just do what he says." Moving backwards with Ray, her unwavering glance masked the fear burgeoning from within. Isabel's eyes locked momentarily with the man from her past. Alex McCormick. The only man she ever loved—and hated.

Chapter One

Snow Creek, Colorado 1986

The brisk fresh air clearly added to Isabel's spirited pace this morning. The horses nickered and snorted as she greeted them all by name.

The barn housed ten stalls, five on either side, and a huge tack and equipment room off to the right of the entrance. At the south end a large door opened into a paddock.

Rounding the corner of the tack room, her arms full, Isabel's striding momentum plowed her into the body of an unsuspecting stranger. She lost her balance and fell backwards, the equipment scattering about her on the dirt floor.

Isabel looked up to see an unfamiliar face regarding her.

"I'm sorry. Are you okay?" His hand extended to help her up. "I couldn't get out of the way fast enough."

"I'm fine." Isabel rose and brushed the dirt from her jeans. Isabel beheld the athletic build of the stranger before her. "I didn't realize anybody else was here."

"I was admiring the horses. Couldn't sleep this morning so I was taking a self-guided tour." He ran his fingers through tousled dark hair. "By the way, I'm Alex McCormick." He held out his hand.

Isabel shook it, matching his grip. "Isabel Medina," she offered. He was at least six to seven inches taller than her five feet four inches. His eyes held her captive. Dark thick lashes contrasted against the blue of his eyes, their color reminding her of the cerulean blue she used to paint the sky.

"Oh, Michael mentioned your name yesterday." As he smiled his eyes did too.

A slight flush crept onto Isabel's cheeks as she recalled Michael's teasing last night.

"I think my friend John asked about you when he saw you working in the paddock," Alex said.

His friend? Why did she suddenly feel disappointed? Lacking in something to say, Isabel bent down to pick up the brushes and combs lying on the ground.

"Here, let me get that." Alex gathered up most of it and followed her to one of the stalls.

"Thanks. You can just toss it there." Isabel indicated a place near the door. They stared back at one another.

"I better get going before I get double time mending some fence." His eyes smiled again. "See ya."

"Sure." Isabel murmured staring after him. She noted his white T-shirt stretched across broad shoulders and the muscular outline of his legs in the faded jeans. His black heeled boots kicked up dirt with each long stride. *The gringo Michael and Joey referred to yesterday?* She smiled to herself thinking about the slight southern accent that echoed in her ears. *Back to work, Isabel.*

❦   ❦   ❦

The white Ford pickup truck rounded the dirt drive, its back tires sliding and throwing up dust. Isabel shook her head. Michael showing off already.

"Hop in back, Izzie. There's no room up here," Michael hollered out through the window. Joey's current girlfriend, Theresa, sat sandwiched in the front seat.

Isabel's eyes widened at the sight of Alex as he hopped down to help her haul the cooler onto the bed of the truck.

"Thanks," Isabel said, climbing in as he gestured for her to go first. She took a seat next to Kenny and felt Alex slide in next to her after he secured the tail gate. She greeted everyone and noticed another new face sitting directly across from her.

"Hello. I'm John Wyatt." His perfectly straight

teeth flashed a charming grin. Straight blond hair stuck out from underneath his baseball cap.

"Isabel. Isabel Medina," she countered.

"I know. Michael told me about you."

Isabel swallowed hard, trying to fight the uncomfortable rush of blood to her face. Avoiding any further exchange, she turned her attention back to Kenny and his sister.

Isabel felt Alex's presence next to her but whenever she glanced his way he seemed lost in thought. Days after their encounter in the barn, she found herself preoccupied with looking to catch a glimpse of him. He was probably one of the best looking guys she'd seen and she remembered those blues staring down at her. Only afterwards berating herself for being so silly. As if he had any interest in her.

As they neared the lake, Michael once again gunned the gas, leaving them to slide around in the bed of the truck. Taken by surprise, Isabel grappled for something to hold onto, missed, and nearly landed in Alex's lap.

His arm grasped her waist as he held tight to the tail gate with his other hand. Laughter could be heard from within the truck as they came to an abrupt stop.

"Sorry," Isabel said scrambling out of the truck. A warmth lingered where Alex's arm had wrapped about her.

Everyone grabbed their supplies and set up camp on a flat spot near the water's edge. Within five minutes they had all stripped down to bathing suits and as usual Rachel screamed at Michael and Kenny not to throw her in.

"Albeit against her will," Alex muttered, as he, along with Isabel and the others waded in gradually.

Isabel smiled to herself. *A sense of humor, too.*

She watched Alex, clad in cut-offs, dive under and come up shaking the water from his hair. The water glistened across his back. His skin already tinted a light golden bronze from working outdoors in the spring sunshine. Isabel quickly averted her eyes when she saw Alex glance her way. *Get a grip, Iz. Stop staring.*

Isabel normally enjoyed the water football game but found John Wyatt's overzealous tackles too much to endure. She told the others she had a cramp in her leg and needed to get out for awhile. No sense in making everyone feel uncomfortable.

After drying herself off she unpacked a sketch book from her pack and started drawing. Deeply immersed in her sketching, she jumped when she felt a tap on her shoulder thirty minutes later.

"I didn't mean to startle you. I called your name a couple of times but I guess you didn't hear me," Alex said as he rummaged through the coolers.

"Game finished?" She closed the cover on her

sketchbook and laid it in her lap.

"More or less. Sorry about John out there. He gets carried away sometimes. I think he thinks the best way to get a beautiful girl's attention is to blind side her first and then get to know her." Alex laughed as he positioned himself on a rock near Isabel.

"I thought it best to just let it go." Isabel's thoughts lingered on his words 'beautiful girl'. His blue eyes once again captivated her full attention.

"These mountains are incredible. We have lakes in Austin but they don't compare to this." Alex's gaze wandered about and then returned back to Isabel. "You can keep on with what you were doing. If you don't mind I'll just watch."

"I don't think I can draw with you watching."

"How about a peek then?" He leaned forward and a grin curved the corners of his mouth.

"Sure, but it's just a rough study right now." Isabel turned the pad for him to see.

"Wow! I'd love to see the finished piece sometime. You're talented."

"Thanks." Suddenly she felt self-conscious about her drawing. She wanted him to like it. "I hope to go to college and study art," Isabel blurted out.

"You should. Are you going to start college this fall?"

"I'm waiting to hear about a grant I applied for."

Isabel got up to get a soda, then returned and sat facing Alex. "Do you go to college in Texas?" As they talked she couldn't help noticing that his T-shirt clung to the still damp spots across his muscled torso. Afraid he'd notice her appreciative appraisal of his physique, Isabel forced herself to keep her eyes on his. Not that that didn't involve some control as well. She could easily get lost in the depth of those blue eyes.

"Yeah. I've been attending the University of Texas but I had a little problem this year," Alex said, shifting his gaze to the ground.

Isabel's curiosity got the better of her. "Problem? Care to elaborate?" A teasing tone laced her words.

"Well, I kind of goofed off this year." Alex shrugged his shoulders. "I let my grades slip and just about got kicked out of school."

"Oh." Isabel's forehead knitted together.

Alex surprised her when he continued on. "It's pretty stupid, I guess. I mean, what the hell was I thinking?" Alex's eyes remained focused on the ground, as if he were talking out loud to himself. "I thought my father was going to kill me." Alex's hand swept through his hair a couple of times before continuing. "But I still think this so-called punishment thing of his isn't quite what he had in mind."

"Punishment?" Isabel asked.

"Punishment. Sentencing. He sent me here to learn a lesson. If I agreed to work here he'd continue to pay for my education. Otherwise I'd be on my own. With some influence from my father the school will allow me to return in the fall."

Isabel looked up to find Alex staring intently at her.

"I didn't mean to unload that all on you. I guess I thought you should know where I'm coming from," Alex offered.

"I'm curious. What exactly does your father expect you to learn from all of this?" Isabel knelt down as she gathered her sketching supplies and stuffed them back in her bag.

"Well I'm sure he thought that working here with these people I'd learn a lesson."

"These people?" Isabel flung the bag on her shoulder.

"Well, I mean, you know, the working...class." The last two words tumbled out before he could stop himself.

"You mean, people like me?" Isabel's eyes flickered. "Mexicans? Uneducated poor people? People who actually have to work to make a living?"

"No, I didn't mean it to come out like that." Alex stood up to face her.

"Oh come on. That's exactly what you meant.

Your father thought working with these poor Mexicans would straighten you up fast and you'd go back home appreciating all you have. Funny how ignorance breeds ignorance." Her last sentence barely audible, but she knew he heard it. Before she turned to go, Isabel noted the prominence of his square jaw as his mouth clamped shut.

She strode to the truck and threw her bag in the cab. She inhaled deeply several times to regain her composure.

People's prejudices invariably struck a chord deep within her. Why did people think they were any better than someone because of their race? Sure she knew there were Hispanics who helped feed the stigma attached to their culture, but she believed that it wasn't their race that made them that way but people's ignorance that kept them there.

Isabel spent the rest of the afternoon swimming and keeping her distance from Alex. However, she did note that he guzzled quite a few beers with his friend John. If his siesta on the ride back was any indication of their excess consumption, he'd be nursing a sweet hangover in the morning. Isabel couldn't help but feel some sort of satisfaction from that.

Later that evening her grandmother Tochita questioned her mood, but Isabel brushed her off saying she'd just gotten too much sun. She was tired, that's all.

Tochita's intuitive nature sometimes drove her crazy. She couldn't hide anything from her, not that she tried, but there were times when she didn't want to tell her everything that was going on in her life. Sometimes she didn't understand it herself.

Chapter Two

On Monday morning Alex made it a point to get up thirty minutes earlier than usual. As he entered the barn he noticed a light coming from inside the tack room. *She's already here.* Alex took a deep breath and took a step into the room but then noticed a mare tied outside a stall at the end of the stable. He walked to the stall and looked in to see Isabel pitching clean hay in a rhythmic fashion. A skill afforded by many hours of practice.

She wore her long dark hair in one loose braid that draped over the side of her shoulder. Her close-fitting jeans were cinched at the waist.

Alex cleared his throat. Obviously startled by the intrusion, she grasped the pitchfork tightly in her hands and turned to face him.

"I hope you don't intend to use that on me." Alex mocked a defensive stance in the doorway. "I know I was an ass on Saturday but I came to apologize."

Alex regarded her unabashed demeanor with amusement. She lowered the fork and rested the handle against her hip, crossing her arms.

"This isn't going to be easy, is it?" Her silence answered his question. "I'm sorry I came off sounding like an arrogant jerk." He noted she raised her left eyebrow. "I know my circumstances are a lot different from yours, and I'm not always aware of how good I have it, but I didn't mean to insult you." Alex moved closer.

Isabel tilted her head down and kept silent a moment before she spoke. He could see her thick dark lashes flutter when she glanced up at him. "Maybe I got a little defensive." Her hand moved to sweep the braid off her shoulder. "Sometimes it's irritating when people refer to us Mexicans as if we're beneath them."

"I didn't mean for it to come out like that. It was a stupid thing for me to say. I guess my father's bigotry has rubbed off on me in ways I wasn't aware of. Really I am sorry. I hope we can start over." Alex extended his hand. "Truce?"

Isabel smiled at him and placed her hand in his. "Sure." As she began to withdraw her hand he held it firmly. "You're not going to kiss my hand are you? You've got polite manners but this—"

Alex laughed. "No, but I would if that would help."

"That's all right. I accept your apology." She tilted her chin down looking at him from the corner of

17

her eyes. "My hand?"

"Well, I was wondering," Alex inhaled before continuing, "if maybe I could buy you dinner or take you to a movie this Friday?"

Isabel's eyes widened. "Uhm. I, I don't know." Her stammering made him realize he had taken her by surprise.

"I know it's a little presumptuous of me to assume that you would even consider it, but I was hoping,...maybe?"

"I'd like that," Isabel replied.

"I mean, we could just do dinner if you don't want to—" A baffled look clouded his face. "Did you say yes?"

Isabel shook her head. "Yeah, but a movie sounded good, too." The teasing tone in her voice escaped Alex's attention at first.

"Well, sure, a movie and dinner. Great, it's a date. I mean it doesn't have to be a date date just a dinner and a movie." He realized he was gushing like a sixteen year old. "I better get to work before I really make a fool of myself." He laughed along with her. "I'll talk to you later then." He let go of her hand and turned to go. He glanced back to see her watching him, a dimple in her cheek deepened as she smiled at him.

What the heck was all that babbling about, Alex? It's not like she's the first girl you've asked out on a date. He hadn't planned on asking her out at that moment but when he'd held her hand it just spilled out. He felt something he couldn't quite understand. Of course her natural beauty caught his eye the first time he saw her, but he liked the passion he saw reflected in her eyes. An energy and spirit that he felt lacking in his own life.

❧ ❧ ❧

Alex joined John at his favorite watering spot. He had his eye on a waitress there who so far seemed to resist John's inexhaustible charms.

"You still going with me to Denver on Saturday?" John asked while running his fingers around the frosted mug of beer.

"Sure. Hopefully not too early. I've got a date on Friday night." Out of the corner of his eye Alex watched for John's reaction.

"No shit? Who?"

"Isabel Medina."

"You didn't waste any time. She's pretty hot. A little young though?"

"I think she's eighteen."

"Well, I guess she's legal," John chuckled. "You might get lucky."

"Hey. It's not like that. She seems like she'd be

a lot of fun. You know, smart, nice, and easy on the eyes."

"Oh no, you're already hooked."

"It's just a date, John."

John laughed. "We'll see."

Alex took John's teasing in stride. They'd been friends ever since grade school. At one time John's parents socialized with his until John's father lost money in several bad investments and eventually they divorced. Alex sometimes felt guilty whenever he saw John struggling to join the same clubs and schools he did. Alex knew John's goals always revolved around making it big, believing once he had money life would be grand.

John volunteered to work at the ranch when Alex explained his father's proposal, figuring it would be a perfect break for him and a chance to make some money.

Things definitely looked better knowing John would be accompanying him. They'd had their share of disagreements but Alex could always count on John's friendship.

The rest of the evening Alex watched with amusement as John did his best to sway their waitress to go out with him. Alex noticed a couple gals smiling and looking his way but his mind was distracted by one particular smile. Isabel's. And the smile remained fixated in his head the rest of the week.

Chapter Three

A local restaurant in town served as their meeting place. Alex offered to pick her up but she convinced him it would be easier to meet him there. Tochita pouted about not being able to meet him first but Isabel didn't want her to scare him off. Tochita's inquisitions were sometimes relentless.

For most of her life, Isabel juggled the sometimes annoying, yet well intentioned, interference she received from Tochita and the Perez family. She knew it was out of their love and concern they felt they needed to be involved in all her decisions but she doubted any man would or could meet their criteria. With Alex she wanted it to be different.

Isabel found Alex standing at the corner of the bar when she arrived.

"I'm sorry I'm so late. It took me longer to get ready than I had anticipated," Isabel offered, without going into her indecisive clothing dilemma.

"That's a relief." His exaggerated sigh puzzled her.

21

"What?"

"I was beginning to wonder if you were going to stand me up as a joke. Like getting me back for last Saturday," Alex replied.

"Oh." Isabel kept her voice low and her face serious. "The evening's just begun and who knows." The flustered look on his face brought forth the laughter she'd been holding in.

Isabel ordered a soft drink as they waited for a table. The crisply pressed denim shirt he wore brought out the darker pigments of his blue eyes. Alex leaned over slightly, propping his arm on the bar as he faced her. Isabel had no choice in the jammed space but to stand close to Alex. Her nose detected the masculine smell of his freshly shaven face. For one wild moment she felt like they were the only two in the room. Thank God she was still able to carry on a conversation.

Impatient with her desire to get to know him Isabel fired questions at him once they were seated. "So tell me about your family."

"Not much to tell. I'm an only kid."

"Okay. What are you going to college for?"

"I'm majoring in business management. I've got about a year left and then I'll be working for my father."

"Well, that's convenient."

"No, it's more like expected."

"Sounds like a sore subject." Isabel pushed the nachos away from her. "Do you and your father get along?"

Alex helped himself to a couple more bites and then moved the plate to the opposite corner. He leaned his elbows on the table and looked directly at her. "Actually I think we mostly tolerate each other. I don't know. I guess you'd have to understand where he's coming from. He grew up poor and worked real hard to get where he is. He expects the same from me."

"But that was his choice. Is that what you want?" Isabel's eyes locked with his.

Alex gave a halfhearted laugh. "You don't pull any punches, do you?" He swept his hand through his hair. "I don't think about it much. My father made it pretty clear from the beginning I'd better go his route or I'd be on my own. A business degree will always be useful later when I pursue what I want to do."

"And that is?"

"Now don't laugh, but I'm interested in landscape architecture. I know it's a far cry from Mr. Businessman but I've been drawn to it for a long time. I love being outdoors and the idea of planning landscapes."

"You sound intrigued by it. Someday you're going to have to give yourself a chance at it."

Alex nodded. "I know." Silence ensued

momentarily as they assembled the fajitas they shared.

Alex took his turn with the questions. "What about you? You live with your grandmother, right?"

"Yes, Tochita, as she prefers to be called. My parents died when I was six." Isabel saw the look of concern on Alex's face. "I don't really remember them. Mostly images. What little Tochita has told me is my mother ran off when she was seventeen, met my father and got pregnant. They lived together for awhile but I guess Tochita convinced my mother to move back home when she found out he was abusing her."

"How'd they die?"

"Tochita says he came and talked my mother into taking a ride with him. He was drunk and lost control of the car, killing them both."

"I'm sorry. It must have been kind of tough not having your parents around."

"I've got the Perez family. I consider them my family. Michael, Joey and Tony, the one who's away at college, are like my brothers. Tochita and I moved here after my parent's death and the Perez family helped us get settled. We didn't have any family in Albuquerque and I think Tochita felt she'd get through my mother's death easier in a new place."

"When Michael heard we were going out he told me your grandmother was pretty tough."

"She can be. But my grandfather died when my

mother was twelve and Tochita raised her on her own.
Luckily her house was paid off and they had some
money saved. Tochita was educated at some of the best
boarding schools in Mexico so she did pretty well man-
aging things. And then came me."

Alex pushed his plate away and concentrated all
his attention on her. "Well, you seemed to have turned
out just fine to me." Alex's grin spread when he saw the
slight flush on Isabel's cheeks.

They spent the next couple of hours talking
about everything and anything. Occasionally ordering
soft drinks to keep the waiter happy.

It was nearly nine-thirty when they exited the
restaurant. Too late to catch a movie. She couldn't
remember when she'd ever had such a good time just
being with someone.

Alex took her hand and turned to face her. "It's
still early. Can we go some place?"

"Well," Isabel wasn't sure where he had in mind.
"There's not a whole lot of night life here."

"I know. I just don't want the evening to end
yet. Can we just walk or something? It's a great night
out."

His beseeching manner caught Isabel off guard.
"That's fine. I'd like that." Maybe he was enjoying
himself as much as she was.

Alex spotted an ice cream shop and pulled Isabel

along with him. When the girl behind the counter asked them what they wanted, Isabel and Alex answered, 'mint chocolate chip' in unison. They became aware of the girl's annoyance with their giggling, which made them laugh all the more.

"There's a small park just over there where we can sit." Isabel motioned to their right.

They found a bench near the middle of the park. Their only light came from a lamp near the street.

Alex sat down next to her, his thigh slightly resting against hers. Not that she minded. He finished his cone first, leaned back against the bench, and deftly swung his arm behind her.

Isabel smiled to herself finishing the last of her ice cream. The quiet and peaceful atmosphere comforted her. "I love the sound of the river." Isabel spoke barely above a whisper.

"I was wondering what that was." Alex whispered back.

"Close your eyes and listen. You can almost see it sweeping along the river's edge and rushing over the rocks." Isabel's eyes remained closed as she tilted her head back, forgetting Alex's arm laid against the back of the bench. She snapped her head back up and felt a flush run up her neck.

"You certainly have a unique way of looking at things," Alex said, his voice low as he leaned his head closer.

"Tochita says it's my artist's eye. She said when I was a little girl I'd take a flower or leaf and examine it, taking in all the details. If you look close enough you can see beauty in the simplest of things."

"I see what you mean." Alex's words drifted into the darkness.

The nearness of Alex and the deep resonance of his voice made her feel light-headed. A compelling desire to turn and kiss him astounded her. What was she thinking? What would he think?

"Isabel," Alex said softly. "Can I kiss you?"

She turned to face him. *My God, he's asking?* Without hesitating she leaned closer and met his lips.

At first slow and precarious, the awkwardness of their lips' initial touch diminished as their kissing deepened. Her mouth willingly yielding to his gentle probing. Isabel felt Alex pull her closer as she placed one arm around him and laid her free hand against his chest. His heart seemed to beat against her palm.

Minutes later she drew back and tried to catch her breath. "I, I need a little air," Isabel said leaving her hand upon his surging chest.

"I'm sorry." Alex slightly relaxed his arm's embrace. "I guess I got a little carried away."

Alex lightly touched her cheek with his fingers then slid them under her chin, tilting her face to his.

"I've really enjoyed our date," he said hoarsely as he bent to kiss her once again.

It was after midnight when Alex walked her to her car. "Thanks, Alex."

"I'll give you a call, okay?" Alex said as he leaned in her open window. "Oh wait a minute. It probably won't be until Sunday evening though. I promised John I'd go to Denver for the weekend."

Isabel nodded. "I'll see you Monday anyway."

"Okay. Thanks for a great night." Alex squeezed her hand and then stood back as she drove off.

Isabel wasn't even sure how she got home. Thoughts of Alex occupied her whole drive back. Even as she drifted off to sleep she could still feel his lips on hers.

🏆 🏆 🏆

By late Sunday evening, Isabel figured she had just imagined her date with Alex. He hadn't called and doubts flooded her mind. *It was just a date,* she kept telling herself. He probably kisses other girls like that. Tomorrow, if I see him, I'll pretend like it was no big deal. That way neither of us will feel obligated.

Chapter Four

By mid-afternoon Isabel broke free for lunch. As she grabbed her sack in the tack room she heard the hinges of the squeaky door close behind her. Before she could turn, hands encircled her waist and guided her back up against the wall.

"What?" her breath caught in her throat. Isabel looked up to see Alex's deep blue eyes smiling mischievously back at her.

"Want to romp in the hay?" Alex's playful tone did its intended job on her. Her firmness of mind had all but deteriorated.

The upward slant of her lips belied the seriousness in her voice. "You're lucky I didn't hurt you for scaring me like that."

Alex raised his arm up and rested his hand against the wall above her. He leaned in close. "I wasn't worried." His husky voice lingered in her ears.

Isabel felt her skin warm as his breath caressed her face. She averted her gaze from those eyes, trying to collect her senses. Tongue-tied. "I, I..." she stammered.

She closed her eyes, the gentle touch of his knuckles brushed the side of her cheek. All the words she had rehearsed—vanished.

"Sorry I didn't call." Alex rested his hand on her upper arm. "It was so late when we got back. I tried to catch you this morning but you hadn't arrived yet."

"It's okay. No big deal." Isabel's eyes remained focused on the base of his neck.

"Are you sure? I honestly thought we'd be back earlier."

Isabel watched as his chest expanded with each breath. She could feel his eyes on her. "Really, it's okay."

"Will you look at me?" Alex asked.

Isabel maintained a straight face as she tilted her head up. She fought the restive urge to touch the lock of hair resting on his forehead. "I only spent half the night cursing you and all guys for that matter."

Alex bowed his head. "Great. I blew it. Would it help if I told you that you were all I thought about this weekend?"

"Maybe." Isabel held her chin erect.

"I did. Every moment. I knew calling you would be torture. Not being able to see you."

Isabel grinned. "Okay. That's enough. You're getting far too mushy for me."

"I'm desperate. Please forgive me." The forlorn

look upon his face brought instant laughter from both of them.

"I will. But don't get on your knees and start begging. I'd really start to wonder about you."

"I really am sorry." Alex's hand remained on the wall above her. "Can I see you after work?"

"Wow, you don't waste any time," Isabel teased, ducking under his arm. "I'd like that."

Over the next few weeks they were virtually inseparable, spending all their free time together. And for once in their lives, Michael and Joey kept their noses out of it, only occasionally teasing her about the rich gringo.

Isabel found herself thinking about him constantly. Loving his smile and his gentlemanly manners. He treated her like a queen and she ate up every minute of it. But the strong attraction also raised some fears she didn't quite know how to deal with. They talked about everything except about their feelings for one another. Sure she liked him, well maybe more than just liked him, but it was the what ifs that kept her up at night.

After a few weeks, Isabel decided it was time he met Tochita. Alex talked to her on the phone but Isabel hadn't let him near her. At first Tochita seemed reluctant to accept the fact Isabel was serious about him. She kept insisting she was too young and his money would interfere and only bring her heartache. Isabel tirelessly explained that Alex was different and the money didn't mean anything. And she was old enough to handle it. Thankfully, Tochita greeted him warmly and only once referred to his money. Alex handled it gracefully and his polite demeanor seemed to win Tochita over.

Afterwards Isabel took Alex on a walk through the back of their property down to a stream.

"Do you think she liked me?" Alex asked, taking a seat next to her on the grassy bank.

"I knew she would like you. It's just Tochita can be difficult."

"You were worried?" Alex's meaning escaped Isabel at first.

Isabel turned to look at Alex. "No, but I guess I was afraid."

"Afraid of ..." Alex held his last word.

Isabel closed her eyes and a moment later opened them to see Alex steadfastly waiting for an answer. "Afraid that maybe it would be too much. That you'd be scared off." Isabel pinched her bottom lip between her teeth.

Alex grabbed both of her hands in his. "Listen, Isabel. I'm not going anywhere. It would take more than your grandmother's inquisition to scare me off. I want," Alex paused, "I want to be with you, Isabel."

Isabel smiled and inhaled deeply. Tears of joy

begged to slide down her cheeks. Her overwhelming feelings for Alex had frightened her. Her heart seemed to be guiding her into unknown territory. An inner voice cautioning her, *don't get too close, you'll get hurt, he'll leave, you'll be alone.* Isabel squeezed her eyes shut, forcing the flow of thoughts from her head. Something told her to trust him, to trust herself. Everything would be okay.

"Is this part of your property?" Alex asked as he pitched some pebbles into the moving water.

"No, this is the Petersen's land. We only have about an acre and they own the surrounding property, about fifteen acres I think. I'd love to buy their land if I could ever afford it. It's a great piece of property." Isabel wrapped her arms about her bent knees. "I want to have some horses of my own. A couple dogs running around. Someday maybe."

"You plan on staying in Snow Creek?"

Without hesitation she answered. "Oh yeah. I love it here. I'd like to do some traveling after I get through college but I'd definitely return here." Isabel's animated face spoke of her passion for her surroundings.

"I can see why you like it here. Colorado is more beautiful than I imagined."

Isabel faltered a moment before asking Alex her next question. What if she didn't like his answer?

33

"What about you? Any other place you'd like to live other than Texas?"

Alex continued skipping rocks across the water's surface. "I like Texas, but—" he hesitated and then turned to face Isabel. "But I'm not tied to it. I think I could probably find a good reason not to stay there." He smiled at her. "You never know."

Isabel's heart skipped a beat. Had she read too much into his words? She didn't think so.

Alex reached over and took Isabel's hand in his, bringing it to his lips and gently placing a kiss on her fingers. Goose bumps rolled up her arm. He pulled her close, lowering his mouth to hers. Their kissing intensified with every second. Alex's restless hand slid up the length of her waist. Isabel's breathing halted momentarily as she felt his hand lightly brush against her breast. An unfamiliar moan sounded from within. Raw emotion tore through her, alarming an unknown part of her brain. Slowly she became aware of Alex staring down at her. He placed a gentle kiss upon her forehead and then along side of her face, down to the lobe of her ear.

"I love you., Isabel." His whispering words struck a chord deep within.

"Alex, I love you, too." She squeezed herself against him. They remained wrapped in each other's arms, eventually resuming their kissing, yet the quick and anxious exploding passion within her frightened her. Alex must have sensed it as well. He looked down at her, his concerned eyes searching her face.

Isabel smiled up at him. "Did you know that you have the most incredible blue eyes?" She lightly ran her thumb across his eyebrow. "Hypnotizing almost."

"Is my spell working?" he teased.

"From the moment we met." Isabel grinned as she pushed him over on his back, pinning his arms down. "Can it be broken?"

"No, it's the first and last one I'll ever cast." Alex half attempted to free himself of her simulated wrestling hold.

Isabel playfully struggled to keep him pinned, thankful for the lighthearted exchange. Her body's response to his touch aroused in her feelings that left her confused and unsettled. Her mind fought to control sensations she'd never experienced before. Surprisingly though, instead of embarrassment she rather liked it. Isabel forced herself to focus on something other than the lingering feel of his hands. *It's too much to think about right now*, she told herself.

Isabel released his arms and before he could react, she tickled his sides and then ran off. Alex caught up to her as they neared the house, assuring her he'd find her weak spot, too.

He already had, she thought.

Long after Alex left, the words 'I love you' rang in her head. She secretly daydreamed about it but never really let herself believe it. To know he felt the same way brought forth an amazing surge of joy. Her face beamed and she wanted to shout it out. *Alex McCormick loves me!* Unable to concentrate on anything else that evening, she decided some painting would help. A painting for Alex. Her blissful mood evident in the way she vigorously wielded her paintbrush against the canvas. Vibrant colors danced at the tip of her brush and from her imagination she created an inviting spot, where trees and flowers filled the space and majestic mountains reigned in the background. Out of Tochita's watchful eye she could let her heart pour forth onto the painting.

🎉 🎉 🎉

Alex didn't know where it came from. It sneaked up on him out of nowhere. At that moment, looking into those deep dark eyes he knew. He loved her. Never before experiencing the depth of what he felt for Isabel. She moved him. Her spirit and her innocent passion for life filled the void in his. He felt whole with her. Connected. The desire to protect and care for her almost innate. Take her places she'd never seen, shower her with gifts she could never afford. Give her the life she deserved. Now he had to find a way to make it work. Somehow they'd be together forever.

Chapter Five

The luxury of privacy didn't come easy for Isabel and Alex. After readying the horses for their ride up to a secluded lake, north of the ranch, both looked forward to some time alone.

They both wore long jeans over their swimsuits. Alex's long legs straddled the saddle and Isabel couldn't help notice how his blue T-shirt outlined the definition of his torso.

A non-verbal competition ensued as they vied for position, Isabel using her expertise to maneuver her horse ahead. She giggled at Alex's frustrated face when he finally caught up with her.

"I let you win," Alex said as he loosened the reins to let the horse graze. He reached over and grabbed her thick braid in his hand, gently pulling her near enough so he could lean over and kiss her. "I liked watching you from behind."

Isabel gave him a sidelong glance. A shiver tickled her inside, her body responding to his words. Her moist lips curved up at the corners. Trying to ignore the assortment of sensations her body was experiencing she turned her attention back to their ride. "Once we climb this part of the path it's only another ten minutes or so. Would you like to lead?"

"That's okay. You're doing fine." Alex winked at her.

Once they reached the clearing near the lake, they let the horses drink and then hitched them to a low tree branch. Isabel spread a large blanket out and watched as Alex unpacked their picnic lunch. He pulled off his jeans before settling himself next to her. Isabel picked at the cheese and cut a couple slices from an apple she shared with Alex. She became increasingly aware of his nearness. Why did it feel as if her heart pounded against her chest whenever his arm brushed against her? She couldn't think of anything to say.

Alex broke the silence. "Iz, I wanted to talk to you about something."

Isabel looked over at Alex and tried to read his face. "What is it, Alex?"

"I think we should talk about us and the end of the summer."

"What about it?" Her casual tone masked her apprehension.

Alex took her hand in his and positioned it on his knee.

"Well, I think we need to make some plans. I

think both you and I need to decide where this is going?"

"Alex," Isabel chewed on her lower lip before continuing, "I don't think we have much choice. You're going back to school and I'll start classes in the fall and we'll write and keep in touch and..."

"Wait a minute. Not so fast. I have something to say about all this, too. I don't want what I have with you to end. You've become a part of my life that I don't want to lose." Alex cupped the side of her face with his free hand. "I'm in love with you, Isabel, and you're not getting rid of me that easy."

Tears sprang to her eyes. At that moment, the disquietude that had unconsciously guided her life shattered when she looked in Alex's mesmerizing blue eyes. He wouldn't leave her.

"I don't want to get rid of you. Not ever, Alex McCormick." She untangled her hands from his and placed them against the sides of his face pulling him closer. They shared a deep and tender kiss.

"We'll work something out, Isabel, trust me," Alex said pulling her up to a standing position. Stripped down to their bathing suits they plunged into the cool water. Holding hands they stood in water up to their necks.

"Isn't is peaceful here?" Isabel asked. "I haven't been up here since last year when this friend set me up on this stupid blind date. We went for a hike and for some reason this guy got the wrong impression about me and started grabbing at me when my friend went off with her boyfriend."

"What happened?"

"Well I had to defend myself, so I jerked my knee between his legs as hard as I could and..."

Alex started laughing. "Poor guy."

"Right." She teasingly glowered at Alex. "If he hadn't been in such pain I think he would have killed me. But he deserved it."

"You're right. But obviously he had no idea who he was dealing with."

"That's right," Isabel countered, aware that Alex's menacing grin meant trouble. "Don't even think about it," she said moving backward. "Please don't tickle me, Alex."

"Oh I won't. I kind of cherish my private parts."

The smirk on his face brought laughter bubbling forth from both of them.

An hour or so passed when Isabel came up behind Alex and clasped her arms about his waist. "It's getting a little cold out here. Keep me warm," she said as she snuggled up against his back.

"I'll warm you up," Alex said, pulling her around in front of him and enfolding her in his arms. After several moments his hand lifted her chin up and he kissed her softly on the lips.

Isabel responded instantly, arms encircling his neck. Alex pulled her up closer as she wound her legs around his hips. Their kissing continued until she realized they were within a few feet of the lake's edge.

Alex made his way to their spot under the tree and Isabel dropped her legs to the ground but didn't loosen her grip about his neck. Alex slipped the elastic band from her hair, releasing the thick strands from its braid. She felt his hand firmly on her back as he dipped her low onto the blanket. Grabbing one of the corners Alex pulled it over to cover them.

Alex's hand lightly caressed the skin on her neck and shoulders. Inexplicable chills coursed through her body. She could feel his lips glide over the delicate skin at the base of her throat.

A delicious pleasure from within took her by surprise. It was as if her mind had separated from her body. His warm breath left its trail on her skin.

His hand eased under her top and lingered on her breast. The pad of his thumb rubbed her nipple ever so slightly. Fire spread down to that spot between her legs. Pressing her body against his, she couldn't seem to get close enough.

With a silent moan her hands began to stroke the smooth muscles of his chest and felt his gasp of breath as her fingers trailed over his belly.

Alex's voice reverberated in her ears. "Isabel. Isabel, we've got to stop."

Confusion wrinkled her brow until his meaning became clear. She looked deep into his heavy lidded blue eyes. "I don't want you to stop." Her voice low and throaty.

"But Isabel," Alex began but Isabel interrupted him.

"I love you, Alex." Isabel watched the creases in his forehead even out as he smiled.

"I love you too, Isabel, but are you sure you're ready for this? I mean, I don't know if—"

"I'm sure, Alex. I'm more sure of this than any-thing else in my life right now." Isabel ran her fingers through his damp hair.

"I know you think you are, but things won't be the same between us."

"You mean you would just use me and then *adiós*?"

"No. You know that's not what I mean." Alex's tormented face relaxed when he saw her lips curve into a smile. "I'm serious, Isabel. I love you and I want you to be sure."

"Alex, I've known since the moment I saw you, my body has known for weeks, and my heart is saying yes to all of it. I want to." Her fingers stroked the nape of his neck. "I want you to be my first." 'And only',

43

silent words she said to herself.

Alex bent his head and kissed her gently until he felt her lips' urgent hunger. Isabel's fingers laced through his hair, unaware of her tightening grasp. The unfastening of her top sent heated sensations to the core of her belly.

Afraid of her body's reaction to Alex's fondling of her breasts, she tensed her muscles at first. Alex slowed his movements and dipped his mouth to the tips of her breasts. Keeping her eyes closed, Isabel allowed herself to succumb to the unique sensations of her body. Her innocent inhibitions melting with every second.

With his mouth covering the dark peaks, he let his finger trace an invisible line down to the top of her bikini bottom. She gasped at the sensitiveness of her skin under his touch. Alex's finger slowly slid back and forth under the waistband before he sought the place between her legs. Her hips pushed against his hand.

Reaching down, Isabel removed her bottoms, watching Alex do the same. Their protective blanket now tangled underneath their intertwined bodies. Isabel's passion mounted beneath Alex's fervent gaze. She traced her fingers along the moist skin of his back and down the sides of his lean torso. Hesitantly finding her way across his hips and to the hardening of his desire. He moaned against her ear and every last bit of modesty dissolved as she grasped him possessively.

Alex raised himself above her and waited as she parted her legs to receive him. "Please tell me if it hurts," he whispered.

Isabel nodded, her eyes smiling back at him. Only for a brief second did she find discomfort. Consuming pleasures spread through her like wildfire, wiping out any remaining uncertainties. Only the need to reach some undiscovered place, to release her from this escalating rush of rapture. It came with such force Isabel heard herself cry out Alex's name.

Alex's body tensed and then shuddered as he found the same release. His labored breathing warm against the side of her face as Isabel delighted in the weightlessness of his body on top of her before he withdrew himself.

Lying on his side, Alex rested his head against the knuckles of his hand and gazed down at her. "You're so beautiful, Isabel." Alex leaned forward and kissed her gently. "I've never known anyone like you," he whispered.

"I know," Isabel smiled beneath his admiring regard, "and I'll never let you forget it."

Chapter Six

Alex pulled the ribbon off and carefully slipped the covering off the easel. He looked back at Isabel who remained near the door.

"Isabel." Alex let out a sigh. "I, I...Wow. It's fantastic." He stepped back and stared at the painting.

Isabel walked up beside him and laced her arm through his. She glanced at him sideways and saw his jaw twitch slightly. "Alex, is there something wrong?" A slight flood of panic washed over her.

"What? No, I love it, Isabel." Alex turned to face her and ran his hand through his hair. A gesture Isabel knew to mean he had something on his mind. "I need to talk to you. About Saturday."

Isabel felt her defenses shoot up. He wasn't going to... "Alex, what is it?"

"I behaved recklessly on Saturday." Alex took her hands in his. "I didn't use any protection. I can't believe I was so stupid."

"Oh, Alex." Isabel expelled a drawn out breath.

"I thought you meant something else." She exhaled again trying to still the trembling coming from within.

"Like what?"

"I don't know, like you were sorry it happened or something."

"God no, Isabel." Alex swiftly took her in his arms. "Don't ever say that! I'm not like that. Don't ever doubt that I love you, Isabel."

"I know. It's just that you scared me. You were so serious."

"But it is serious, Isabel. We don't need that kind of complication right now. I'll carry condoms with me from now on but we can't take that chance again. I blame myself. I know better." Alex took her face in his hands and kissed her lips. He then moved to her ear and whispered. "Even if you do drive me wild."

Isabel grinned. "Well, *Señor* McCormick, don't get any ideas. Tochita's waiting for us."

ۄ   ۄ   ۄ

The mid-afternoon sun shone brightly down on the fiesta crowd. Both he and Isabel had agreed to help out in the morning and then enjoy the food and entertainment on their own in the afternoon. He had even recruited John to serve up soft drinks.

"I'm starved, Isabel. Let's eat first."

"Okay. This way." Isabel led him to a covered tent housing tables and a buffet line serving hot and cold food. Filling two plates Isabel explained the filled corn husks were tamales, and the chilé she smothered on the beans might be a little hot for his taste. Alex grabbed foil wrapped tortillas and followed her to a table. He listened with interest as Isabel conversed in Spanish with an elderly man and woman sitting nearby.

"Were they wondering who the new boyfriend was?" Alex asked, nudging her shoulder with his.

Isabel's eyes twinkled with an impish gleam. "Maybe."

"Yeah, I see all these guys who flirt and stare at you." He kept his voice low and looked around to make sure no one was listening. "All past lovers, right?"

"Get out of here," Isabel said, playfully swiping at his chest with the back of her hand. She kept her voice barely above a whisper. "You know you're my one and only."

Alex reached over and pecked her on the cheek. "I know, but I like to hear you say it."

Finishing their meal Alex looked up to see a swarm of girls heading their way. With his help they persuaded Isabel to come and start up a dance. Alex followed as far as the stage but then they directed him to wait while they donned their costumes. Isabel rolled her eyes at him. 'Just you wait' she mouthed back to him.

The amused smile he gave her stayed plastered on his face when she returned with the other girls, all dressed in brightly colored skirts that swirled about them as they moved to the music.

Alex watched with fascination as Isabel held the skirt up in both hands fluttering it about her rhythmically as the girls followed suit. Isabel's bare feet seemed to move as if she were dancing on a cloud. Her blazing eyes attested to the joy she derived from the ritual.

My God, she's beautiful, he thought. Alex never imagined feeling this way about someone. Unable to explain it in words, he felt as if something beyond his control linked Isabel to him. Even though the summer would come to an end, he knew that this wouldn't. He wouldn't let it.

After another energizing dance, Isabel escaped from the platform and came to stand next to Alex. Her breath came in short spurts and her chest rose and fell beneath the ruffled blouse.

Alex eyed her appreciatively, her skin glistened. "Do you get to keep the costume? Maybe wear it for me later?" Alex's baiting remark got him a steely stare from Isabel. He couldn't hold it in any longer. He burst out laughing as she smiled and shook her head.

They stayed and watched several dances put on by children. Alex found the Dance of the Little Old Men to be his favorite. At first he didn't understand why the boys came out dressed to look like old men with walking sticks. But moments later he burst into laughter, along with everyone else, when they would suddenly leap up and start dancing energetically and just as quickly, they became weak old men again. Everyone got a kick out of one little boy who couldn't have been over six. His timing was off but he stole the show when he tried to mimic the moonwalk.

As the remaining rays of sunshine fell away the temperature dropped. Isabel accompanied Alex to his car so he could grab his sweatshirt for her. He personally wanted the chance to be alone with her for awhile.

"I have something for you." He pulled out a rectangular shaped gift box and handed it to her.

Isabel slowly untied the ribbon, then tore away at the wrap. A sterling silver charm bracelet lay enfolded in tissue paper. Isabel pulled it out, depositing the box on the hood. "Alex, it's wonderful." She examined the three charms dangling from it.

Alex explained each one. "This one's a paint palette, to remind you that you're always an artist. And this one is in the shape of Texas to remind you of me, and this heart is for us." Alex turned it over in her hand. "It's engraved. It says, 'Isabel and Alex—Always.'"

"Alex. I love it." Isabel reached up and hugged him tight.

Alex leaned against the front fender and gazed

up into the dusky sky, marveling at the brilliance of the sun setting over the mountains.

Isabel found her usual niche within his arms. "Did you have a good time, Alex?"

"Actually I did."

Isabel leaned back slightly and looked up at him. "So us Mexicans aren't so bad?"

"Isabel." The creases in Alex's forehead wrinkled together.

"I'm just kidding, Alex. I don't hold it against you anymore."

"Anymore? You forgave me, remember?"

"I remember."

"You know, Isabel, I've learned a great deal about myself since meeting you. I've learned something about people that I used to keep at a distance because of my father's planted prejudices. People that live and breath just as I do and yet seem to have a better time doing it." Alex chuckled. "You're incredible, Isabel."

As it neared time for the fireworks display, they decided to stay put.

Alex's next words took them both by surprise. "Come with me to Texas." They seemed to avoid the subject of his leaving at the end of the summer...she because it was inevitable...he because he didn't want to leave. Being here seemed far removed from the expectations awaiting him back home. His father, school and his future. A future he definitely wanted to share with Isabel.

"What?" Isabel jerked her head back in complete surprise.

"I can't leave without you."

"Alex, we've talked about this. You're going to finish up school and then we'll decide. It just gets too complicated any other way."

"But maybe it'll work. Who knows?" He brushed a stray lock of hair from her cheek.

"Exactly. I don't want to become a burden or resentment in your life. We love each other and we'll just wait and see."

Isabel's calm voice intensified the warmth enveloping his soul. "Why are you so levelheaded? You're the female, aren't you suppose to be crying and begging me to stay?"

"What good would that do?" Isabel said, tracing her finger along the wrinkles of his shirt. "What if you said no and then where would that leave me? Answer me that."

Alex bent and kissed her gently on the forehead. "I wouldn't say no," he whispered into her ear.

Before she could respond, a boom sounded and a shower of bright colors lit the sky above them. Alex could feel her sigh against his chest. Isabel turned in his arms, leaning her back against him as he positioned his hands on her crossed forearms. They both joined in with the faint oohs and aahs heard throughout the crowd.

Chapter Seven

John raced up the steps, cursing the third time he'd tried to catch the telephone before the caller hung up.

"Hello?" John answered, nearly out of breath.

"Please hold for Mr. McCormick please," a female voice replied.

"Alex?"

"No. Mr. McCormick, this is John Wyatt. Alex is out right now."

"I see. I've been trying to reach him all week. What the hell is he doing there?"

"Well we've been putting in some hours, and plus with his girlfriend he's not here much."

"Girlfriend?" Silence hung in the air like an oppressive band of humidity.

"How long has this thing been going on, John?"

"Well they met right after we got here but..."

Mr. McCormick cut him off. "I see. I didn't send that goddamn kid up there to screw around. Listen here, John. I'm going to make this worthwhile for you.

Do you know what I mean, son?"

"I'm not sure, sir." His palm felt damp against the telephone handle. John listened intently to Mr. McCormick's instructions. It sounded simple enough. He ignored the guilt creeping into his thinking. Mr. McCormick offered him something he couldn't refuse. An opportunity he never would have gotten on his own.

Luck played into his hands. He'd been repairing some rotted rafters in the barn and one day noted Isabel's morning episode. Observing her from afar, he watched her place a hand on her stomach and hold onto a railing to steady herself. Another piece of the puzzle fell into his lap when he overheard her telling one of her co-workers she was leaving early for an appointment.

John followed. He knew his answer when he saw her disappear through a door. The doctor's name etched on the frosted glass, his specialty, obstetrics, emblazoned below his name.

John had done his job and Mr. McCormick said he would take care of the rest.

      ♤   ♤   ♤

Isabel's drive to the ranch seem endlessly long. The small jaunt from where she parked would give her some time to think about how she was going to tell him. But as she walked along the dirt path a grip of fear and doubt seized her. Wait. She needed time to think about this. The next couple of days she'd be gone and this would give her the opportunity to think it through. Some way of making it work. She knew Alex loved her enough but she wanted to make sure she presented their predicament with some solid plan. A plan that would hopefully get them through this without any resentful feelings or misunderstandings.

Turning back she didn't hear the sound of the door banging open as John's narrow eyes watched her from the top step.

Isabel talked to Alex briefly in the morning before she headed out to help transport a couple of horses to eastern Colorado. Noting Alex's strained voice, Isabel felt an uneasiness descend upon her. Did he know?

"Alex, is something wrong?"

"No, we'll talk when you get back."

"If there's something bothering you, tell me now. I don't want to keep wondering if something's wrong." Isabel's insides knotted up. Recently she noticed a tension between them. Neither wanted to deal with the fact that in a couple of weeks things would be different. He'd be gone.

"I have to leave Saturday."

"Saturday? Why? I thought school didn't start for another three weeks."

"It's my father. He's adamant I get back now, says there's some things he wants to go over with me."

"But didn't you tell him about us."

"Isabel, he didn't leave it up for negotiation. I just didn't think I should push it."

"Fine, Alex."

"Isabel, don't. I don't want to fight about this."

"I'm not fighting. If that's what he wants, well, then I guess we don't have any choice. I'll see you when I get back. Bye." Click. She heard 'I love' before she cut him off. Isabel took several deep breaths to calm herself down. Tears formed. Her emotions seemed so close to the surface. Alex's fear of standing up to his father was about the only thing they disagreed on. And right now it only added to her anxiety. How would Alex's father react to having a grandchild?

Chapter Eight

Alex's hand lingered on the pay phone. If she left over an hour ago she'd be here by now. Maybe he misunderstood her. Got the time wrong. He'd wait a few more minutes then try again. He sat on the park bench and watched some kids play on the swings.

They shared their first kiss here. They went so far as to refer to it as their park. He smiled to himself. Meeting Isabel had changed everything. He would have never imagined he could feel this way. So complete when he was with her. And even though they'd had a couple of disagreements lately, he didn't feel threatened by it. He reasoned the tension between them was because of having to be apart. At least he had something to look forward to now. His last year of school and then he'd work for his dad and he and Isabel would be together again.

He hadn't told his parents about Isabel but he thought maybe his mother suspected something when she asked about the beautiful painting he mailed last week. Alex didn't go into details but told her a friend had painted it for him. His dad would come around. He'd see to it or tell him to go to hell.

If he let himself think about it too much, he could feel his heart tighten, imagining what it would be like without Isabel's radiant face there to greet him. Whether she smiled or frowned at him he found it to be the most beautiful face he'd ever known. A face forever etched in his mind.

✓ ✓ ✓

The afternoon sun glared across the windshield. Isabel started her car and opened the windows to let whatever breeze there might be cool the interior. She wanted to make the best of their time together but she couldn't help but notice the tension in her body. Keeping this all inside and knowing Alex had to leave had taken its toll.

As she drove along the road, her mind somewhere other than her driving, she felt a mild cramp in her abdomen. She looked down. A dark spot stained her yellow shorts and she felt a sticky fluid between her legs. "Oh no. What's wrong?" Panic gripped her. The steering wheel jerked left. She tried to correct it. The oncoming truck swerved. She heard the crunching of metal against metal before her head struck the windshield and screams filled her ears.

🏵 🏵 🏵

Half crazed by nightfall, Alex drove over to her house and again waited there until he could no longer contain his anxiety. Where could she be? He tried the Perez home. No answer there.

He decided to return to the ranch and wait. Surely she'd call.

By 7:00 a.m. the next morning Alex, unshaven and clothes wrinkled, knocked on Isabel's door once again. He saw a light on but several minutes passed before the door opened.

"Mrs. Medina. I need to see Isabel." Alex rubbed his knuckle against the lid of his red rimmed eyes.

Tochita remained on the other side of the screen door. She clasped the edges of her black cardigan with one fist, the other hand still holding the handle of the door. "Alex. I'm sorry." Tochita's unwavering stare seemed to go right through him. "She's not here."

"Where is she? She was supposed to meet me yesterday and never showed up. I came by last night and no one was home." Alex's throat felt dry.

"I don't know what to say. She's gone, Alex."

"Gone? Gone where?" Alex's pushed his shoulder's back.

"Yesterday. I thought she told you."

"Mrs. Medina, what are you talking about?" Alex resisted the urge to yank open the screen door.

"She left yesterday with Michael and Joey to pick up their brother Tony. I know you are leaving but I thought you two must have said your good-byes already. She won't return for another three or four days."

Alex stared at Tochita's wrinkled face, yet his glassy eyes never detected the nervous twitch of her bony jaw. "Thank you, Mrs. Medina. I'm sorry to have bothered you."

"I'm sorry, Alex." Tochita swiftly closed the door and leaned back against it. The rush of air from her action ruffled the folded check on the table. Twenty thousand dollars. The beginning of Isabel's future.

The engine idled. Alex stared out through the dusty windshield, his eyes burning and heavy with fatigue. The voice in his head tried to reason with his confusion. Was this Isabel's way of saying good-bye? Just take off so she wouldn't have to do it face to face? Doubts began flooding his thinking. He didn't deserve this.

He cranked his stereo up. Tires spinning, dirt and rocks flying, he shifted into first gear. A cloud of dust followed him down the road until he hit pavement.

Alex spent the next several hours riding through the canyon trying to make sense of it all. Unfortunately it only fed his growing anger. Only one thing to do. Go home. Alex's jeep skidded to a stop in front of his door.

John's lopsided grin suggested that the bottle of beer in his hand was not his first.

"Get that ass-o-nine grin off your face. Are you packed? I'm leaving now," Alex said as he took the steps two at a time, not waiting for an answer.

John scrambled in behind him. "I thought we weren't leaving until tomorrow."

"Change of plans. No use sticking around here." Alex gathered up his two duffel bags and began stuffing his belongings in. "She didn't call, did she?"

"Uh, you mean Isabel? Uhm, no." John picked at the label on his beer. Sweat beaded on his upper lip. "Is that why we're leaving now? What she do? Demand money or something?"

"John," Alex stopped for a moment and turned to face him. His clouded eyes narrowed. "We're not going to talk about her, you hear me. I don't want you to mention her name or anything about her or you're walking."

"I'll get my stuff." John pulled his bags out from under his bed, glancing briefly at the disconnected phone cord underneath the small nightstand. "Ready, Alex."

"Load the jeep and we're outta here. Got any beer left?" Alex asked as his eyes swept the room one more time. He walked over to the nightstand and reached down.

"Alex," John half shouted, "I'll put some cold ones in the cooler."

"Huh? Right. I think I left a book in here." Alex pulled open the drawer and withdrew his book tossing it into his bag. "Let's hit the road." As the jeep made the turn onto the highway, an uneasy feeling came over Alex. He had no reason to doubt Mrs. Medina. Even though at times she tried to manipulate Isabel he felt she only did it out of love. Maybe he should wait, go back. Isabel probably did this out of fear. Really how could he blame her? She was the one staying. Alex's fingers absently rapped against the gear shift knob. Okay. Just accept it Alex. Go home and cool off. Things will look better tomorrow. Once he got home he'd call, they'd talk and everything would be as it should.

Chapter Nine

Denver, Colorado February 1998

Alex tackled the last of the boxes, one of the three his mother stored in the attic for him after he moved to his apartment in Austin. Pulling out its contents the sight of the colorful painting hit him like a ton of bricks, the vivid hues jumping off the canvas, begging for his attention. He traced his finger along the painting's texture. His contemplative musings shattered by the rhythmic rap on the door.

"Hi. I'm Liza, your neighbor next door. My husband Stevie met you the other day. Here." Liza handed him a foil wrapped plate as she stepped up to the threshold. "Banana nut bread. I wanted to welcome you to the neighborhood."

Alex invited her in since she didn't seem to be in a big hurry to leave. "Come in." Alex took the bread from her and watched as Liza perused the interior of the living room.

"Nice stuff you've got." Liza walked over to stand in front of the canvas. "Well look at this. That's a gorgeous painting. Where you gonna put it?" Liza looked around as if trying to find a spot for it.

"I'm not real sure. I just unpacked it, and uhm, hadn't really given it much thought." Alex tried to ignore the uncomfortable surge of emotions barreling to the surface.

"Isabel Medina? Never heard of her but I like it. Looks like a place right out of the mountains."

"Actually it is. She's from Colorado."

"No kidding. Do you know her?" Liza bent to examine it up close.

"I did. It's been awhile." Alex sighed.

Liza's hazel eyes seemed to look right through him. "I see. Well, I better scoot out. Gotta take my dog out for her walk and get back to work. Nice meeting you, Alex." Liza retrieved a slip of paper from her pocket. "Here's our number. Just call if you need anything."

"Thanks, Liza. I will." Alex saw her to the door. Wheeling around, Alex stared at the picture leaning up against the door frame. Isabel. Twelve years and the images still clear. God how he had loved to watch her paint. Splatters on her workshirt and a smudge or two of color always ending up on her face. Passion fueled her art work. Did she still paint? He wondered. Actually he wondered about a lot of things. And decided at that moment he needed to get out for awhile, he'd been unpacking boxes for a week now. Time to take a break.

The highway's winding path seemed different yet the same. The earlier assault of feelings diminished as he drove. For a time he refused to let himself recall anything about that summer. The painful memories burned long and deeply. But with time the ache within lessened and he promised himself to let it go. It just wasn't meant to be.

He took the familiar exit. Snow Creek. Maybe he'd grab a bite to eat and then head back down. The Bear Creek Tavern's full parking lot seemed a good indication of decent food. Taking a seat at the end of the bar he ordered chicken enchiladas from the bartender. After the great meal he decided on another beer before heading out. The crowd thinned and Alex surveyed the interior, decorated with a rustic mountain feel. Alex's eye stopped on some paintings mounted on the opposite wall. Something so familiar. A horse grazing in a pasture of wildflowers. A homestead in the background. The ranch. He needed a closer look. Inspecting the corner for her signature, he had to stop himself from touching it for fear someone would see this desperate act.

Impulsively he bought it. The owner, somewhat shocked, revealed it wasn't really for sale but Alex's offer swayed him otherwise. It amazed him how the sight of her art work evoked such charged emotions.

Why after all these years? A longing still so strong and encompassing he felt the urge to act on it. To ask where he might find her. To see her and make sure it hadn't all been a dream.

Not in a million years did he imagine he'd return to Colorado. He had agreeably settled in Austin, worked for his dad, and eventually earned his degree in landscape architecture. But when he told his father his intentions to have his own business, that cut the final strand of their relationship. The memory of that day remained fresh in his mind.

"You're a screw up, Alex! A daydreamer!"

"I'm not asking for your permission. It's what I want to do."

"You'll be back. Begging me to bale you out. Just like that goddamn mess in Colorado."

"What mess?" Alex gripped the sides of his chair.

"That damn Mexican girl who had you suckered in. Couldn't see it coming, could you? A girl like that is only looking for one thing. Money."

Alex approached his father's massive desk and for a fleeting moment saw fear reflected in his father's eyes. "What the hell did you do?"

"I took care of it. Paid her twenty thousand dollars."

"You what? Why?!" Alex's clenched jaw spit

67

the words out.

Alex's father stood and faced his son eye to eye. "To keep your ass out of trouble. Trapped by some spic who played you for a fool."

"It's a lie."

"I've got the canceled check to prove it. Never heard from her again, did you? Think about it, Alex."

Alex pounded his fist against the desktop. "I don't have to. That's it! You'll never interfere in my life again!"

And that was the last time he saw his father. No matter what, no matter if he failed, he'd never again seek his father's help. Thanks to Ted Robert's referrals and some money inherited from a great aunt, he'd had enough to start up his own landscape business. Here in Colorado and far enough away from the domain of his father.

He could still remember the incredible rage flooding through his veins. Hatred and pain intermingled with shear confusion. The unanswered letters. The disconnected phone number. He'd spent months making himself crazy. Yet to think of what his father did and the idea that Isabel accepted these terms tormented his soul. Would he ever know the truth? Discovering the answers scared the hell out of him. Not wanting to admit to the betrayal that lurked there.

Alex glanced at the restaurant owner's business

card after he loaded the picture in the back seat. Tony Perez, Bear Creek Tavern Restaurant and Catering. Too much of a coincidence. Enough. Dwelling on the past would never do him any good. Funny though, how fate slapped you in the face when you least expected it.

Chapter Ten

Snow Creek, Colorado   June 1998

Isabel could hardly contain her elation after Tony's call. Immediately after work she drove over to the restaurant.

Tony's manager greeted her at the door. "Hi, Isabel. Congratulations."

"Thanks, Eric. I can't believe it."

"Why not? You're talented. But be careful, Tony might start charging you a commission."

Isabel laughed. "Is he busy?"

"He's in back. I'll get him for you."

Isabel perched herself at the end of the bar. The usual bartender acknowledged her and poured her a soft drink.

Tony appeared with a broad grin on his face. "Don't trust me to hold onto your money?"

"I just had to come and see if it was true."

"Of course it's true. The couple didn't even try to bargain. Took it right off the wall. Here." Tony handed her the envelope with cash inside. "Now aren't

70

you glad I talked you into putting price tags on your work? If people know they're for sale they'll buy."

"I know, I thought the first one you sold in February was just a fluke."

"Right. Let me buy *la artista* some dinner. Would you like the special?"

"That'd be great. Thanks Tony." While waiting, Isabel sipped her drink. Out of the corner of her eye she realized someone had taken the seat next to her.

"Hi. I didn't mean to eavesdrop but are you Isabel Medina? The artist on the wall over there?"

Isabel blushed, still uncomfortable with calling herself an artist. "Yes."

"They're wonderful." He extended his hand. "I'm Ray Calhoun."

"Nice to meet you." Isabel noted his pleasant smile and the cleft in his chin, a la Kirk Douglas. His soft brown eyes an added asset to his attractive face. Short blonde hair, almost too neatly tousled, seemed fitting on this well-dressed man.

Tony served her dinner but couldn't join her because of some employee problems. He gave her a warning glance when Ray offered to keep her company.

"I take it you two are more than friends."

Isabel missed his insinuation at first. "You could say that."

"Oh." Ray swallowed the last of his beer.

"No, he's not my boyfriend. We grew up together, as close to family as it gets. He and his two younger brothers treat me like the sister they never had. Lots of teasing and practical jokes."

"Good, I mean, I didn't want to start anything."

Isabel found herself enjoying the light exchange with this engaging man. He wanted to know about her work and her family and listened with interest. But the most surprising thing was that he made her laugh, really laugh. How long had it been since she'd let herself enjoy the company of a man? Especially someone she'd just met and hadn't been fixed up with. A complete stranger. A man who, before they parted ways, somehow talked her into giving him her number.

Swept off her feet was the only explanation she could give Tony later when he asked about the three hour dinner. All his brotherly advice and cautionary warnings disregarded. The prospect of seeing this man again excited her. She only hoped she hadn't misread his attraction towards her.

On her way out Tony introduced her to his new part-time bookkeeper/part-time kitchen help. Lena Gomez.

Isabel immediately noted Lena's unfriendly and reserved tone. But maybe she'd only imagined it. Her head was in the clouds right now anyway. Today seemed almost perfect.

Ω Ω Ω

Isabel burst in on Tochita, clad in her robe, pouring herself a cup of coffee. "Tochita, I sold another painting!"

Tochita pressed her close. "That's wonderful, *hita*. You'll be rich and famous any time soon."

"I don't know about that but it feels good knowing someone likes it enough to want to buy it." A glowing smile remained on Isabel's face as she added milk to her coffee cup.

Joining her grandmother at the kitchen table Isabel listened half-heartedly while Tochita attempted to carry on a conversation with her. It was the name of her mother that caught her attention. "I'm sorry, Tochita. What did you say?"

"I was just thinking how much you remind me of Angela."

"You never told me that."

"The same eyes, and at one time she had your spirit, too."

"You mean before she had me?"

"Before she met your father. She had dreams, too. But he ripped them from her. I don't know why she let him. I tried to tell her." Tochita's agitation apparent in the way she gripped her cup.

"She was young, Tochita. Sometimes when

73

you're in love it's hard to see the truth."

"Yes, but sometimes when you're old you can't see it either." Tochita pulled a tissue from her sleeve and dabbed at the corner of her eye. "I'm very proud of you, Isabel. I know it hasn't been easy having *un vieja* raise you. I'm sorry for all the mistakes I made. I hope someday you'll forgive me. I only wanted the best for you because I love you."

Isabel smiled and squeezed Tochita's hand across the table. "I know, Tochita. I love you too." Isabel went to the sink and rinsed her cup out. "I've got a ton of papers to finish up for the last week of school, Tochita. If you need me I'll be in the studio."

As she walked outdoors Isabel's head reeled from Tochita's candidness. It wasn't like Tochita to talk about her mother, or anything in the past for that matter. Isabel never got very far and finally learned to accept it as Tochita's way of avoiding any painful memories. Isabel did wonder what brought it on, though. She promised herself to pay closer attention.

A few years back Isabel converted the garage into a makeshift art studio. Giving her more space to work on projects. After she started teaching she included an office in the loft above to work at after school.

If the paintings continued selling, she'd be able to devote the whole summer to painting and not have to worry about taking a summer job. Her art supplies took a big chunk out of her income. Tochita's small government subsidy helped somewhat, but the past year the house had needed several repairs and a complete overhaul of the electrical system. Sometimes it seemed she'd never get on top of it. But at this moment she didn't care. Things were looking up.

❧ ❧ ❧

The closed window shades blanketed the room in darkness. In the corner of the room a television flickered, the volume low. Ray's shoulder held the receiver to his ear as he pulled out a pad of paper and flipped on the desk lamp.

"Yes, sir. I've met the Medina woman. She gave no indication of knowing the gal when I casually mentioned her name.

"What now?" The man's gruff voice irritated him.

"Give me a couple more days to snoop around. I'll contact the old lady next."

"You better find something or else I'll find someone who can." The phone went dead.

Ray didn't like threats but considered himself use to them. Men like that lacked the insight needed for a job like this. And that's why they hired him. Patience, precision and preparation. Armed with an arsenal of background research on the Medinas he had plenty of weapons to play with.

Tracing her here was easy but now came the hard part. Fishing her out. The gold digger had no idea what she'd stumbled upon. The disc information clearly worth more than what they offered her. Obviously she wanted to unload it for some quick cash. Computer technology proved a lucrative area to work in, no matter what side of the equation you were on.

As a rule he never got directly involved with anyone on a job. Unfortunately he hadn't counted on Isabel Medina's lovely visage. Or her beguiling innocence. He found her confidence stimulating and yet he detected a delicate vulnerability beneath the surface. A mystery to unlock.

Chapter Eleven

Bells hanging from the glass doors of the drug-store rang again. Ray glanced up and then back at his watch again. He arrived twenty minutes before their appointed time. This way he'd see her first. The magazine rack positioned near the door offered the best spot to observe people coming and going on the street corner. Ray rehearsed his plan while waiting. He had to make her trust him. Promise her he'd keep it all to himself.

Ray watched as Tochita Medina scanned the sidewalk outside. Dressed in a dark floral dress and black cardigan, she stood clutching her black leather purse.

"Mrs. Medina. Hello," Ray said, walking up beside her.

"What? Ray?" Tochita's eyes squinted beneath the folds of aging skin. She tried to hide her surprise at seeing him. "I'm here doing some shopping."

Ray grinned. "No. You're here to meet me."

"I don't understand." Tochita pulled her purse tight against her midsection.

M. *Louise Quezada*

"Let's talk over here." Ray motioned to a spot over near a bus bench. He knew he had to keep it simple and non-threatening. No one would be the wiser to a man having a friendly conversation with an elderly woman. Reminding himself to smile occasionally so as not to raise any suspicions.

Tochita hesitated, glancing about her before yielding to his wishes. "What is it you want?"

"Mrs. Medina, I don't mean you any harm. I'm only interested in some information regarding a Selena Olivas." Was that a flicker of surprise in her eyes?

"I don't know what you're talking about."

"I think you do. I know she contacted you. Maybe sent you something in the mail?"

Tochita nervously shook her head. "No."

Surprised at her reluctance Ray tried another tactic. "I know for a fact that Selena Olivas knows you and that she's here in Colorado."

Tochita took hold of the bench, settling herself down on its edge. "I don't know where she is." Tochita's long bony fingers held a tight grip on the bag lying in her lap. "I only received a letter from her but that's all. I can't help you." She rose from her seat.

Ray placed a hand on her forearm, making sure he smiled. "I don't think you're telling me all you know." His grip tightened.

Tochita jerked her arm away, holding her shoulders erect. "Stay away from me and my granddaughter. I will not stand for your bullying me." Angry eyes flashed back at him. "Leave us alone." Tochita's surprisingly quick pace left him standing looking after her.

Dammit. The old bitch definitely screwed up his plans. He hadn't figured on her refusing to give him what he wanted. Maybe he'd have to scare her a little. Make her see he wasn't taking no for an answer.

Ray sprinted to his car parked in a back alleyway. Within moments he saw the beige Ford up ahead. The way she clutched her purse made Ray suspect she had something with her. The highway practically deserted, gave Ray the freedom he desired. The car lurched forward under Ray's floored pressure on the accelerator. A game of cat and mouse might make her see things his way.

۞ ۞ ۞

Isabel hung up after the twelfth ring. She could no longer concentrate. Where could she be now? No answer at the Perez's. No doctor appointments had been scheduled and nowadays Tochita rarely drove herself anywhere. All day long she had an odd feeling. Something wasn't right.

The last couple of days Tochita's dramatic mood swings left her worried. Yesterday she found Tochita's room in disarray. When she offered to help, Tochita reprimanded her like a child and explained they were her private papers. Isabel complied with her wishes and left it at that.

Things changed right after she started dating Ray Calhoun. Tochita appeared to like Ray from the beginning. Always inquiring about what they did or where they went. Admittedly, the relationship had progressed quickly but Isabel felt comfortable with it. Ray respected her opinions, and his keen interest in her life seemed genuine. Flowers or small gifts greeted her on a weekly basis and for once she let herself enjoy the special treatment.

Something else must be bothering Tochita. She had to go home, she'd take her work with her and finish up there.

"Tochita? I'm home." Isabel walked in the back door leading into the kitchen. Utter stillness. Isabel checked the answering machine. She grabbed hold of the desk. A strange voice spoke. "Ms. Medina, This is County Memorial Hospital. We found your number in a Tochita Medina's purse. Please call..." Isabel inhaled deeply. Her finger's fumbled on the buttons. A cloud descended upon her. Her body functioned yet she seemed separate from it. A voice confirmed that a Mrs. Medina had been admitted earlier. No further information would be allowed over the telephone. Sheer dread enveloped her.

Isabel reached the hospital in a daze. A lost and distracted expression remained etched in her face as she asked for assistance. Third floor. Isabel walked into the corridor, unaware of the Perez family approaching her from the left.

"Isabel," Tony called out, taking her into his arms.

Isabel struggled to be released. "Where is she? What happened?" But the despair in their faces told her what she already feared. "No, no," she wailed. "Please no, it can't be." Tony and Michael caught her before she collapsed. Moments later she found herself in a small room, a cup of water being offered, Tony's sad face staring back at her.

"Drink this, Isabel."

She nodded and complied, her eyes fixated on his mouth. His words simple and slow. "Tochita was in a car accident. She died instantly. There was nothing they could do. I'm sorry, Isabel." Isabel buried her face in his chest and sobbed.

She cried for days. The arrangements. The rosary. The funeral. Nonstop crying. And through it all she had the Perez family by her side and Ray. Ray was always near.

Isabel dragged herself through the next week. The full impact of her loss hit every time she entered the back kitchen door. Expecting to see Tochita moving about and singing those old Spanish tunes. Like a tiny part of her brain still didn't know she was gone.

One week after Tochita's death the call came. "Ms. Medina, this is Detective Shelton from the police department. I was wondering if I could come by this afternoon and ask you some questions concerning your grandmother."

"Sure," she answered with squinted eyes, confusion muddling her thoughts. Isabel hung up the telephone. Her eyes remained transfixed upon a spot on the wall. The nagging doubts she had kept at bay cropped up into her consciousness.

Isabel relayed her concerns to the detective whose soft-spoken manner set her at ease immediately. Tochita rarely went out and had no reason to be on that road. What made her lose control of the car? The detective told her they would rule the accident a homicide. The skid marks indicated she swerved to miss something and it appeared that someone else had entered the car after the accident. The glove compartment was pried open and her purse dumped all over the seat but money and credit cards lay on the floor. He assured her they would pursue all avenues.

Like a swelled dam in need of release, Isabel felt

some tension drain away. Inevitably she knew she had to accept Tochita's death but now maybe her brain could make some sense of this ungraspable tragedy.

Ray responded to her call without delay, bringing her a full course meal, a bottle of wine and a single rose to grace their table. His concern in this newest turn of events enlivened Isabel's growing affection for Ray. He offered to help her go through Tochita's personal effects but respected her need to do it alone. Ray's presence offered her the perfect distraction from the loneliness she felt consuming her.

After dinner, snuggled up on the couch watching television, Ray and Isabel's playful kissing became increasingly impassioned. The three glasses of wine enhancing her weary body's response. Ray's almost rough handling of her excited her, diverting her thoughts away from the anguish encircling her heart. His hands moved over her with an urgency that took her by surprise. She didn't care where it led. She needed him.

Within moments he brazenly undressed her and pressed her down on the bed. His hands roamed freely across her breasts and boldly between her legs. Barely stopping long enough to finish their intended provocation. Hastily he slid on top of her, his vigorous thrusts leaving her less than satisfied. After reaching his peak he pleasured her with his fingers, appeasing her physically, but the intimacy she associated with making love seemed distant and forced.

Isabel squeezed her eyes shut to stop the flow of memories fighting to be released. Flashes of blue eyes staring back at her with such tenderness. She shook the images from her head. A little voice inside chided her for sleeping with Ray so willingly. *My God*, she thought, *I'm thirty-two years old, a grown woman. I care for this man and love will surely follow.*

Ray aroused her again in the early morning. His manner gentler and more affectionate yet something in the way he dominated their lovemaking troubled her. She ignored the small sign of foreboding tugging on the outer edge of her consciousness.

Chapter Twelve

Denver, Colorado   August, 1998

After tonight she could get on with her life and really start living. Lena flipped on the small desk lamp in Tony's office. Not taking any chances, she'd download the information onto Tony's computer. Precautions were always something Auggie insisted on. Never trust anyone, he told her.

Lena didn't miss him much. But following his death she realized she missed the financial 'schemes' allowing them to get by without having to work a stupid job. But luck seemed to be on her side. Maybe Auggie put in a good word from up above.

The married man she seduced one night bragged about the information he stole from his employer. Important security access codes for a number of large corporate computer systems. Disgruntled with his boss he decided to utilize the information for his own gains. 'You'd be surprised, honey, how many people would pay for this stuff. These companies have vital information important to the world of patented technology. The future of the computer age.' After their drunken interlude she hatched a plan. The guy never saw it coming. With Auggie's connections she had herself a fake ID and a chance at striking it rich.

Lena feared the old lady's death meant they were getting closer. Fortunately she'd already retrieved the disc from Tochita Medina. She had to dump it soon. Finding a buyer took some time but when she did they agreed to her demand of one hundred thousand.

In a rush to leave Albuquerque, the only out-of-state address she had on hand was Tochita Medina's. And it had served its purpose. The old woman's reluctance to meet her not a surprise considering they'd never actually met before. Without a doubt though, Tochita knew of her existence and agreed to meet privately in an out of the way location. A meeting Lena approached cautiously. No open-armed welcome, but then, Lena only wanted one thing and Tochita agreed to hand it over on one condition. That Lena leave and never contact her again. Fine by her. How they discovered the Medina connection, however, baffled her.

۝ ۝ ۝

"I don't trust her." Ray's voice remained low as he looked around him, the convenience store parking lot deserted at this early hour.

"I don't either," the man replied. "But we have no choice right now but to follow through. Once we have the disc then you can take her out. Be prepared, Ray."

"I always am." Ray hung up. Tomorrow it would all be over. Half the money up front and the rest later. Giving him time to take her out, an accident or suicide. Ray hadn't decided yet. No hint of foul play - that's what they paid him for. She'd join the lover he'd already taken care of. Ray laughed to himself. He hadn't failed yet.

۞ ۞ ۞

The Rockies game went into overtime, and glancing at his watch Alex almost hoped the party would be over by the time they arrived. Who was he kidding? Ted Robert's parties never ended early. The fact Tony Perez catered the party produced a case of nervous anxiety distracting him all evening. He knew curiosity would get the best of him. And there was always the chance Tony would recognize him from buying the painting. Okay. Now or never.

Alex walked through the party as if a cat prowling about. Aware but not really seeing. Searching for just a glimpse. And then he spotted her. The dark hair swept up off her neck, her comely profile outlined in the dim light. The tomboy girl of twelve years past definitely a woman now.

Alex recognized Tony and watched as he entered the house, leaving Isabel by herself. *Okay, now's your chance.* But his timing fell short. Tony promptly returned and Alex realized they were leaving. No. He had to see her, talk to her. To look into her eyes and find the truth.

Following behind he observed the two join another couple across the street. The next scene played out like some B-movie in fast forward mode. And within minutes she was gone.

"I'm going with you," Alex said running to keep up with Tony.

"Who the hell are you?"

"I'm Alex McCormick. Isabel and I, we knew each other a long time ago." Alex crossed to the passenger's side of Tony's car. "I want to help."

❂ ❂ ❂

Ray pushed Isabel through the driver's door into the passenger seat of his black Pontiac Grand Am. The tires squealed as Ray floored the gas pedal.

Isabel's heart beat rapidly as she stared back at the gun resting on Ray's thigh. Helpless. Powerless. Emotions born of an incredible fear threatened to unnerve the center of her existence.

"Ray," Isabel started, "what's this all about?"

"It's just some business I had to take care of. It doesn't concern you."

"What? You've got a gun and kidnapped me. This is insane." Isabel's voice reached an octave or two higher as she fought to keep the trembling inside under control.

"I don't take any chances and the disc Selena stole is worth a lot to the people who hired me to locate her."

"Hired you? What does that mean?"

"You don't need to know any more than that."

Anger boiled in her veins. "Let me go, Ray. I won't do anything to stop you."

Ray snickered before he spoke. "Babe, I'm really sorry about all this. I'll make it up to you. I promise. And I'm sorry about my call earlier. I just didn't like the idea of you being without me."

Disgust curled in her belly. A feeling of dread permeated every inch of her body.

"Goddamn it! The bastard's following me!" Ray hollered out with both hands clenching the steering wheel.

Isabel turned around to see Tony's car keeping a safe distance behind her. Seizing the opportunity, Isabel grasped the handles of her square shaped purse and took a swing. The bridge of his nose bore the brunt of her aim. Blood dripped profusely from his nostrils. The gun slid to the floor as Ray slammed on the brakes. His hands frantically grabbing for her. Isabel felt her jacket tear. One final tug and she escaped his grasp.

Chapter Thirteen

The straps of her sandals dug into her feet as she ran. The passenger door opened. "Tony?"

"Isabel, get in!"

Flinging her body into the car, Tony took off, swerved around the corner, speeding through several lights until he felt sure they'd lost Ray. "Isabel, are you all right? What happened? Did he let you go?"

"He got upset and distracted when he saw you following. I hit him with my purse and his nose started bleeding. Thank God you were there, Tony, I don't know what..." Isabel faltered as the reality of her circumstances began to set in. Adrenaline surging through her veins.

"Thanks to Alex's quick thinking we were able to catch up with you," Tony said, repeatedly glancing in the rear view mirror as he drove down side streets.

Isabel's mind froze. *Alex?* She rotated her head slowly. Alex's face emerged from the darkened interior of the back seat. His eyes held hers until she turned away. A tangled web of thoughts filled her head.

Reluctantly, one by one, teardrops glided down her face. Her body's heightened sensitivity giving way to sobs.

Tony reached over and clasped her hand. "It'll be okay, Iz."

"What are we going to do?" Isabel asked as she tried to regain some composure.

"We're going straight to the police station. Ray's still out there and dangerous."

Isabel nodded in agreement and remained quiet the rest of the way. The silence in the car almost deafening. She could feel his eyes on her. His presence overwhelming. After all these years, the pain she buried so long ago trying to surface. No, she wouldn't let it, she'd gotten over him and moved on.

A Detective Winters huddled them into a conference room. All too aware of Alex's nearness, Isabel kept her distance, sitting at the opposite end while they waited. With her artist's discerning eye Isabel regarded the kindness of time to his handsome face. The boyish youthfulness replaced by a more sculpted face. His smiling eyes crinkled slightly at the corners. Their color deeper. His tanned complexion enhanced by the black knit shirt defining his still broad chest. A pager sounded and suddenly Isabel became aware of her preoccupation. Alex's distracting presence only added to her overwhelmed state. *Pull yourself together,* she scolded herself.

For the next hour they tried to fit some pieces together. Explaining what they knew, which amounted to hardly anything at all. The police were able to determine that Lena Gomez was also known as Selena Olivas from New Mexico and wanted in connection with a murder there. Isabel felt a rush of unsettling qualms after she realized how little she knew about Ray. She didn't know the name of the company he worked for, he was always vague when she asked about his family, and he never mentioned knowing Lena. How could she have missed all this?

Detective Winters tried to assuage Isabel's concerns. "Men like him master the qualities of a charmer in order to deceive people. Believe me, you're not the first or the last to fall prey to this kind of person."

"Think about it, Iz, didn't he seem a little too good to be true?" Tony pointed out.

Tony's plausible statement struck a nerve she'd neglected to recognize. Isabel nodded in agreement but still couldn't seem to get rid of the doubts plaguing her. She just wanted to go home. But the idea got shot down by everyone in the room. Too risky.

"I've got a suggestion," Alex interjected, "since this Ray knows nothing about me why not stay at my place?"

"No," Isabel blurted out, shaking her head at Tony.

Tony ignored her plea. "He's got a point. I'll stay with you, too. At least for tonight, Isabel."

Isabel noted the brotherly tone and knew it useless to argue. But she tried one more time when they reached Alex's house. "I don't want to do this, Tony."

Tony placed his hands on her upper arms. "Isabel, look at me. You're not safe until they catch Ray. You don't have any choice right now."

Isabel entered the house with trepidation lurking in every corner of her mind. She forced herself to appear casual, but this involved significant restraint considering the fact her insides were knotting up by the second.

Flipping on the light, Alex turned and let them pass. "I'm going to run next door for a minute. I'll be right back."

Tony and Isabel walked into what appeared to be his living room. Isabel turned and shook her head at Tony.

He raised his hand. "I'm too tired to argue with you."

"Fine." Isabel positioned herself on the arm of a leather chair.

Tony remained standing, taking in the surroundings. "So that's Alex McCormick?" Tony's question implied more than he was asking.

"In the flesh, Tony." Isabel's dark eyes flashed

warnings in their depths.

"If looks could kill, Isabel." The stinging exchange halted as soon as Alex reappeared.

"I thought maybe you'd want to change into something more comfortable." Alex handed Isabel some folded clothing. "Why don't you take my room, I put clean sheets on this morning."

"Thanks but I'll sleep out here." Isabel retorted.

"I think you'll be more comfortable in there. I have a sleeper sofa in my office and Tony can use the sofa out here."

"Sounds great, Alex." Tony chimed in with a sidelong glance aimed Isabel's way.

"Fine." The exhaustion settling in every inch of her body drained her of any further defenses. She just didn't care at this point. Resisting the urge to slam the door, she gently pressed it closed and leaned against it. Isabel perused the room. A king size bed dominated the small but cozy space. A dresser, filled with trophies, and an assortment of antique tools took up one wall. A whimsical painted night stand graced the corner with books piled high on top and near the floor. Isabel sat on the edge of the bed, placing the borrowed clothes next to her. Fatigue took over. Leaning back against the pillows, she closed her eyes.

❀ ❀ ❀

"Did everything go as planned?" the voice asked.

"Yes sir," Ray adjusted the bandage across his nose. "Is the disc information verified?"

"Yes, it's all there. Now all we need to do is finish this business. Do you understand?"

"I'll take care of it." Ray hung up the phone. Selena certainly wouldn't go anywhere until she got the rest of her cash. His contacts showed no arrest record for her in the past twenty-four hours.

Ray's expertise included careful scrutiny of all angles. However, Selena's simple mind misled him. To think all this time she worked for Tony. Right under his nose. He'd think differently this time.

Isabel had been another story. A part of him said to just leave it be. But he couldn't. Her attack surprised the hell out of him. He actually got excited thinking about it. He needed to see her, to make her understand. But first things first.

Jotting down a couple of leads, Ray began the methodical procedure of eliminating leads or clues. Obviously Selena had changed her name to Lena Gomez, enabling him to find out her most recent address. He'd scour her place when he was sure the cops would be gone. Maybe he'd get lucky again and she'd leave another address behind, like the overnight delivery receipt for Tochita Medina he fished out of the garbage. It didn't take long to uncover the connection.

Ⓠ Ⓠ Ⓠ

Selena spun herself around in the middle of the large hotel suite before sitting down to the huge room service lunch. She'd gotten a kick out of the room service waiter's polite and subservient manner. 'Where would you like it, ma'am? Can I pour your wine, ma'am? Is there anything else I can do for you?' Selena was beside herself.

Settling down to lunch, Auggie's words filled her head. 'Someday I'll find that bitch. She took what was rightfully mine and she'll pay for it.' His speech, always slurred from the whiskey, still rang clear in her ears. She resented this fixation of his. Why couldn't he just be happy with her? A small time hood with one scam after another, Auggie's prison terms did nothing to thwart his plans on hitting it big. She was there in the end. His liver eaten up by the years of alcoholism. She'd finish it for him now.

Selena dialed the number scribbled on a matchbook cover. This time she finally got a voice. "I want the rest of my money," she demanded. "I can't get a hold of Ray Calhoun, but that's not surprising."

"What are you getting at, Miss Olivas? Mr.

Calhoun has instructions to pay you since everything has checked out."

"Well, considering the fact that the police are looking for him, he's not at the number I was given."

"Police?"

"Yes, the police. Your goon's libido got the better of him. He kidnapped Isabel Medina. Now he's wanted and I don't really want to go near him."

"We weren't aware of any problems. We'll take care of it and you'll get your money. Give me your number and—"

Selena quickly objected. "I don't think so, mister. I'll call you tomorrow and tell you where to deliver the rest. But keep Ray Calhoun away from me." Selena's finger depressed the receiver button and then waited for a dial tone. She called the bank and received instructions on how to wire money to her account there. After Ray's crazed behavior she wouldn't trust any of their people.

Selena laughed out loud. Isabel deserved him.

Chapter Fourteen

Isabel sat up. Her night of restless sleep produced bizarre dreams and unreal images. Eyes heavy with fatigue stared back at her. Removing the pins from her hair, she combed through the thick tangled mess. Using a tissue she wiped the smudges from beneath her eyes and splashed some cold water on her face to freshen up. The shower, with its neat shelf of bath products, looked inviting but there was no way. Too personal.

The house seemed quiet. Could she be the only one awake? No, the fresh smell of coffee led her to the kitchen where she found Tony and a woman talking.

"Good morning," Isabel interrupted.

"Iz." Tony crossed the room. "Are you doing okay?

Isabel nodded. "The coffee smells great."

"Isabel, this is Liza Adams. Alex's next door neighbor." Tony continued after they acknowledged one another. "Alex had an appointment this morning and I've got to go and pick up some things so she's going to stay here."

Isabel's jaw clenched but she maintained a smile. "I'm okay by myself. I don't want to inconvenience anyone."

"Oh it's no problem, I'm free all morning." Liza assured her.

"It's settled, Isabel. Alex shouldn't be much longer and I'll be back in less than two hours. Then we'll figure out what we need to do next."

Isabel walked with Tony to the door. "You're in danger, too, Tony. Ray might come after you."

"I've got that covered, Isabel. I hired a security guard for the restaurant until they catch him. I know this is tough on you but with this lunatic running around we can't take any chances. I just feel better knowing you're with someone, okay?"

"Okay, Tony. Can you at least take me home later to get a change of clothes?" Isabel watched Tony nod as he made his way down the walk.

In the kitchen Liza poured Isabel a cup of coffee and gave her an expectant look indicating she wanted her company at the table. Isabel obliged, Liza's crooked smile too friendly to ignore. But awkward silence filled the air between them.

Fortunately Liza jumped right in. "Did the clothes not fit? I can maybe find something else."

Isabel looked down at her wrinkled clothes. "I fell asleep before I could try them on and this morning it just didn't feel right. But thanks."

"I understand. You've been through an ordeal. I can see you probably just want to get home and put your own things on."

"Yes." Awkward silence again.

"You're the painter, aren't you?"

Geez, did Tony tell this Liza her life story? "Actually I'm an art teacher in Snow Creek and paint on the side."

"You should give up the teaching. Your paintings are beautiful."

Isabel's forehead creased. "You've seen my work?"

"Sure. Alex has two of your pieces."

"What?" Isabel's coffee sloshed over when she accidentally banged her cup against the table.

"You know, the two in his office." Liza motioned for Isabel to follow. "With you two being old friends I figured you knew." Liza flung the door open.

Isabel gasped. The painting Tony sold last February hung behind a large wooden desk. Turning to her left she spied the other one. A vertigo like sensation seized her. She needed air. Balancing herself against the door frame, Isabel inhaled deeply several times.

"Are you okay, Isabel?" Liza's hand reached out for her forearm. " I think you better sit down."

"Yeah, I just got a little dizzy is all."

Liza brought a glass of water to Isabel who reclined back upon the sofa in the living room. "Here, drink this. Maybe you need to eat something."

"I'll be okay. Thanks, Liza."

The back kitchen door opened. Isabel tensed.

Alex's smiling face greeted them both. "Hi. Everything okay?"

"Poor Isabel here got a little light-headed."

"I'm fine. Just tired." Isabel interrupted, hoping to keep Liza from saying anything further.

"Did Tony leave?"

"He said he'd be back in a couple hours." Isabel made her way back into the kitchen, looking for her coffee cup. Liza and Alex's voices out of earshot as they remained in the other room.

Through the windows Isabel could see a small iron table and chairs situated on a brick patio. An inviting spot with an assortment of flowers filling clay pots of every size. Graceful curves and lines edged the garden beds as perennials overflowed with blooms. *Alex's handiwork*, she wondered? Isabel lost herself in the peaceful setting, unaware of Alex's presence behind her.

Alex cleared his throat. She turned to find him closer than expected. His citrus-like cologne penetrating her nostrils. The desire to flee came instantaneously. She bit down on her lower lip to stem the tide of turmoil threatening to unnerve her.

Alex spoke first. "Isabel. I know this whole thing has been difficult for you but I hope you know I'm," he paused and laughed quietly. "Actually I don't know what I am. I wish I knew where to start." Alex ran his hand through his hair.

Isabel winced at the sight of this familiar gesture. Her fingers tightened around the coffee mug. "Why did you buy the painting?" The question came out of nowhere.

"Liza said you seemed a little surprised." Alex folded his arms across his chest and shrugged his shoulders. "It just happened. One day I took a drive and stopped for some lunch, not realizing it was Tony's place, and I saw it up there. I always appreciated your talent."

Isabel cast her eyes downward, all too conscious of his blue eyes staring at her. Those same blue eyes that haunted her deepest dreams. Shivers slid up her spine, her body reacting to his close scrutiny and she had no power over it. *Keep your wit, Isabel.* "So how long have you been in Colorado?" Isabel moved to the kitchen sink to empty her cup.

"Since after the first of the year. I started my own business here."

"Landscape architect?" Isabel asked, feeling grateful for the change of subject. "I noticed your backyard."

"My testing ground actually, until I can find some land. Tony said something about you teaching art?"

"Up in Snow Creek at the junior high."

The polite exchange of conversation continued until the telephone rang. Alex answered. "Sure, she's right here."

Isabel reached for the phone and noticed his hand brushed against hers. "Hello? Yes. I'll be there. Thank you, Detective Shelton." Isabel's face paled.

"What's wrong?" Alex's concerned eyes searched her face.

Isabel swiped at the tears filling her eyes. She swallowed hard trying to get the words out. "That was the detective on Tochita's case. He thinks Ray was involved." The tears swelled in her eyes. "He wants me to come to the precinct and talk with him." Her head throbbed at the exertion of keeping it all in. The room spun, her vision diminished as her legs buckled, only the sense of strong arms catching her eased her delirium.

Chapter Fifteen

After her momentary fainting spell, Isabel excused herself to go lie down and rest. The feel of his arms holding her illuminated a faraway place deep in the recesses of her heart. A place she tried to forget and push aside. A place she wouldn't allow herself to dwell on any longer. The pain she endured after that summer took an enormous time to heal. To live through it and go on required every ounce of strength she had. And she wouldn't let it happen again.

At the sound of Tony's voice she emerged. "Tony, you're back. Detective Shelton needs to see me but I want to go home first and look through some of Tochita's stuff. Maybe we'll find something."

"Alex filled me in. He's going to ride with us."

Isabel's eyes flashed. "Sure, why not?" She grabbed her purse and stormed out to the car, taking a seat in back. Tony would get an earful the minute she had him alone. Treating her like some defenseless moron and involving Alex in this whole mess added to her already agitated state.

Like some detective on a police show, Tony made her wait with Alex until he checked her place out. After five minutes she decided she'd had enough. With Alex on her heels Isabel entered her house and went straight to her room. "I'm taking a shower and changing clothes." The door banged behind her.

She picked out a pair of jeans and a white short sleeve top and headed to the adjoining bathroom. Moments later steam filtered out the door as she opened it up to clear the room. Wiping the mirror dry she proceeded to apply some fresh makeup and style her hair. She felt human again when she joined Alex and Tony in the kitchen.

Tony's grin greeted her. "Better now?"

Isabel ignored his sarcastic tone and pulled a key out from a desk drawer. "I want to look in Tochita's filing cabinet in her closet. Maybe I can find something to help." Both men accompanied her to Tochita's room, left pretty much the same as when she was alive. So far Isabel refused to change anything. Too soon to relinquish Tochita's things to just memories.

Switching on the overhead light, Isabel pulled out the top drawer. Neatly filed bank statements and household account information filled the green folders. As well as a deed to the house and other miscellaneous documents. In the bottom drawer Isabel discovered a large square box beneath a manila envelope. Neatly folded inside the box lay a faded sweatshirt. Isabel's eyelids closed slowly as she processed this discovery. Her face flushed under Alex's regard but she refused to acknowledge him. Tucked inside the box was another large envelope with Isabel's name handwritten across it.

Tony withdrew the contents of the manila envelope. "Look at this. It's a letter to Tochita from Selena Olivas." He read it out loud. "We better take this with us and get out of here. I don't think it's safe."

Isabel insisted on packing an overnight bag and reiterated her plans to stay at a hotel. No one argued with her.

🏵 🏵 🏵

Tony went to find Detective Shelton. Alex took the seat next to Isabel. Watching her sweep some stray hairs off her forehead Alex noticed a faded scar extending across her right brow. He would have remembered that scar. Realizing how every feature of her beautiful face remained true to memory. The almond shaped eyes and the fullness of her lips, all carefully preserved in his mind. What could he offer to erase the tension from her face?

"I was sorry to hear about Tochita. You must really miss her." Alex watched as Isabel nodded in answer. "I don't really know what your relationship with this Ray Calhoun was but it must be hard to think he might have had something to do with her death."

Isabel turned slightly. "More than you can imagine."

He knew, almost instinctively, how alone and frightened she was. The pout of her lips, the blank expression in her eyes, the fear beneath the brave exterior. At one time he had memorized every gesture, every sign, every aspect of her. And with astounding force they all emerged into his awareness once again. Tony's voice interrupted any further thoughts as he called them over to Detective Shelton's desk.

"I'm trying to piece together a bigger picture concerning Mrs. Medina's death. We have reason to believe that her death is somehow connected with all this." Isabel went over the police report on Tochita's death with Detective Shelton.

Alex observed Isabel's intense expression as she grappled with what the detective explained. His natural response confounded him. The need to protect her still there after twelve years. Yet uncertainty slinked its way into this thinking and fueled a need to find out the truth. To put the past to rest once and for all.

"We haven't been able to find out much about this Ray Calhoun. All his background information was false. Not surprising though, considering. Can you remember a name or anything associated with his work?"

"No." Isabel shook her head trying to recall something, anything. "Wait, I don't know if this will help but his car had a sticker on the back. I remember the initials MMI because it's my initials backwards."

"MMI is a big computing firm. My father use to do business with them a couple of years ago." Alex offered.

Isabel handed Selena's letter over to the detective. "We found this in Tochita's papers. It doesn't say much other than the fact that she's coming to Colorado and will look her up. The part about retrieving something might be the disc Selena handed over to Ray."

"This is a good start. We have to figure out the connection and go from there." Detective Shelton arose from his seat and walked to the door. "As soon as we know something we'll get in touch. Meanwhile, Miss Medina, keep a low profile. Don't go anywhere near Snow Creek or any other place you frequent. He's a paid hit man and will probably stop at nothing to clean up any loose ends, which means you."

Alex couldn't help but notice the color drain from Isabel's face as she listened to the detective's eerie words. For a brief second he wanted to grab her by the shoulders, peer into her soulful eyes and tell her he'd take care of everything. That she was safe with him. But he had no right. Alex watched as Tony's arm rounded her shoulders and escorted her to the car.

Thankful for the seat in back, Alex grappled with the growing apprehension inside. How did he begin to placate this uneasy feeling he couldn't quite understand?

❦ ❦ ❦

Who the hell was this guy? He'd never seen him before. Ray recalled the stranger from last night. He had panicked when he heard him approach calling out Isabel's name. Ray viewed their visit from behind the towering shrubs near the back of the barn. A hiding place he'd found whenever he needed to see her. His hand held the small collapsible binoculars he always brought with him. They'd never suspect him here and he always managed to remain undetected, walking a couple of miles via the Petersen's vacant property.

Just seeing her appeased his agony. Images of her naked body lying next to his haunted him. Her supple breasts, soft to the touch, her skin smooth and taut beneath his hands. Isabel's inexperience and slight modesty increased his sexual appetite. He'd have her again.

But business first. Selena proved to be more dangerous than he anticipated. Her call set in motion a chain of events he'd make sure she'd pay for. Reassuring his employer took some doing though, and he wasn't quite sure it worked. He'd have to be on his toes now. Hunt her down and put an end to this absurd game of hers. His distraction with Isabel cost him some time but he always came out on top. This time would be no exception.

Chapter Sixteen

Tony pulled into Alex's drive while talking on his car phone. He silently motioned for them to go in without him.

Isabel followed behind Alex until she heard her name called out. Liza was wildly waving from the end of the driveway. "Yoo-hoo Isabel. I want you to meet my Mocha."

Isabel smiled as she realized Liza meant her dog. Reaching down to rub behind the golden haired dog she saw the dog's full teats. "Did she have puppies?" Isabel asked, recognizing the signs after working the ranch for so many years.

"Yes, six of them about four weeks ago. I promised Alex he could pick one out but he said he did-n't think he'd have time for one. You should come and see them. When you get the chance, that is."

"I better not. I doubt I could resist an adorable puppy right now." Isabel laughed quietly.

"Any news yet?"

Isabel shook her head. "No, not yet. I should

get going in. I've got some things to look through. See you later, Liza."

Tony was still on his phone and when she entered the house she could hear Alex's voice coming from his office.

Plopping the box and envelopes down at the kitchen table, Isabel withdrew the contents. Along with Selena's letter was a faded newspaper birth announcement for a baby named Selena Olivas. Born in New Mexico nearly ten years after her own birth. Only her birth mother was named. This proved Tochita knew Selena somehow. Was it an old friend she knew when they lived there? Selena never gave any indication she knew me, only that she seemed to dislike me. Right now Selena held all the answers.

Tony interrupted her thoughts. "Isabel, I've got to meet with Ted Roberts and another guy and get this thing rolling. I'll be back as soon as I can."

"Tony, let me go with you. I'll wait in the car."

"Isabel, I know this whole thing is upsetting and inconvenient, but think about it. If Ray killed Tochita, you're in danger too, and this is the best place for you right now." Tony glanced behind him before continuing. "And I know this thing with Alex is uncomfortable but maybe it's time you grew up and dealt with it.

"What?! I did deal with it and I don't need it thrown back in my face."

"Whatever. I've got to go. I'll call you when I'm finished."

She wanted to tell him don't bother but kept it to herself. They were both under a lot of stress and she was tired of arguing with him. She knew he only did it out of concern for her.

Turning her attention back to the pile, a flash of a summer's evening jumped to mind as she lifted the University of Texas sweatshirt from the box. Something tumbled out from the folded material.

Isabel reached for the small white box. Her fingers slowly lifted the lid off. A shiny silver chain peeked out from beneath yellowed tissue paper. She picked it up and watched the three little charms dangle from their links. Her charm bracelet. Isabel's eyes closed as she clutched the bracelet to her chest. All these years and she thought Tochita had gotten rid of this stuff to help her get over Alex. Why had she kept it? Was Tochita's contempt of Alex a pretense?

Isabel turned at the sound of footsteps behind her, she jerked the bracelet behind her back. Too late. Alex saw the sweatshirt spread out across the table. His face unemotional as his eyes searched hers. Their gazes held steady.

The silence became unbearable. "I didn't," Isabel stopped and averted her eyes. Her palms felt damp. Alex walked to stand in the kitchen, his back to her as he braced his hands on the counter. Isabel stared at his back, his muscular arms flexed as he gripped the edges. She exhaled as quietly as possible wishing she could just disappear.

"I feel like I'm walking on eggshells here. We're two adults and I think we should be able to talk about this."

Isabel stood to face him. "There is nothing to talk about. As soon as Tony gets back I'll leave and you can get back to your life."

"It's that easy for you?"

Isabel felt her throat go dry. She stuffed her hands in her pocket to hide their trembling. "It doesn't matter. It was a long time ago. We were young and things just didn't turn out."

"Yeah, but don't you ever wonder why?"

Why was he pushing? "Alex, it took me a long time to get over you. I spent years wondering why but I finally just let it go. I don't know what good it will do to talk about it." Avoiding his gaze Isabel looked down at the table. Her eyes squinted in confusion. A partially covered letter addressed to her lay underneath the sweatshirt. The familiar handwriting sent goosebumps all over her body.

"Isabel?" Alex walked over next to her and followed her gaze. "My letters," he whispered.

Isabel's shoulder's dropped. "I didn't know."

"What do you mean?"

Isabel reached for the envelope. Her fingers cautiously traced along the opened seal line, she pulled out one of the letters. Tears coursed down her cheeks. Short but to the point. *'What happened? Please call if there's any chance. I still love you. Alex.'* My God. After that summer, hope upon hope, she dreamed she would hear from him. Searching the mail for a sign and it never came. And now she knew why. Tochita.

Alex's hushed tones penetrated her deep thoughts. "You never got them, did you?"

Isabel glanced at him. "No. I don't understand. Why would Tochita do this to me? She knew how much..." Isabel turned away. Walking over to the french doors she pressed her forehead against the glass. Everything she believed to be true now knocked out from under her. A base of lies feeding itself.

"I'm sorry, Isabel."

She felt his light touch upon her shoulder. So familiar. So utterly familiar she had to restrain herself from falling into his arms. No. It still didn't change things. Not after all these years.

The phone's ringing startled her. Alex answered. His voice grew louder as he spoke. "We'll be here," he said, before hanging up. "That was Tony. They found Selena shot in a hotel room."

Terror struck. Her eyes darted back and forth.

Where could she go? He'd find her next. She could sense it. "I have to get out of here." Isabel rushed through the room, but Alex's hand grasped her upper arm.

"Isabel, don't. Just wait a minute."

"I can't. I'm ..." The words stuck in her throat.

"I know." Alex's deliberate and slow movements eased her panicked state. He enfolded her against his chest, his hand gently rubbing her back. "I won't let him hurt you, Isabel."

Isabel leaned back and looked up into the wondrous depth of his eyes. Their sincere warmth dissolved something inside.

"Please trust me." Alex's words trailed off as she laid her head against his shoulder. She felt safe.

Chapter Seventeen

A light rap sounded on her door. It must be room service again. Oh how she enjoyed this. And tomorrow morning, she'd be on her way to another life. Selena opened the door. Ray's hand jammed in between the door's opening before she could slam it shut. She tripped backwards as he entered.

"Ray," she said swallowing hard. The blood draining away from her face. "How'd you find me?"

Ray chortled. "What idiot checks themselves into a posh hotel and uses her real name? You're too easy. The police give you too much credit or else they'd have found you, too."

"What do you want Ray? I thought," she stopped herself.

"You thought what?" Ray's taunting tone turned her insides upside-down. "That you'd get away with that little phone call you made this morning?"

"Ray," Selena cowered back another couple steps. A wild look flashed in Ray's eyes. "I just want-ed my money."

"And you thought they'd give it to you." Ray's crude laugh echoed in the room. "I can't believe you really thought you'd get away with it."

The ugly grin on Ray's face set Selena in motion. She came charging at him but he was ready. He grabbed her wrist and swung her to the floor.

"Let me tell you something, bitch. They were never gonna let you live anyway. I work for the people you stole it from. I'm paid to clean things up."

Selena's eyes widened. It had all been a set up. The reality of her situation came too late. A slim barreled gun pointed down at her. Selena threw her arms up in self-defense. "I always finish my job." Blip. The force of the silencer knocking her back against the carpet. Darkness clouded her vision and then nothing.

❦ ❦ ❦

Tucking his gun in the back waistband of his trouser he looked around to make sure he hadn't disturbed anything. Not that it really mattered anymore. The police were after him and his now ex-employer surely had someone on his tail. Only one more thing to do and then he'd disappear. In this line of work one stayed prepared at all times. Money and passport always ready when the time came.

His departure hinged on seeing her one last time.

Isabel filled some primal need within him. An obses-sion that obscured his rational thoughts. He knew he'd crossed a big obstacle when she gave in to her sexual passions and let him into her bed. Of course he'd taken advantage of her grief but she seemed quite satisfied. A derisive grin played upon his thin lips.

      🏵 🏵 🏵

"None of it makes sense. What would Tochita have to do with Ray and Selena?" Isabel asked as they convened in the living room with Tony.

"You know, right before Tochita died she mum-bled something like 'she's evil like him'," Tony replied. "I kind of forgot about it. It didn't make any sense but maybe she was referring to Ray and Selena. It's too much of a coincidence too that they're all from New Mexico."

"What did Detective Winters say about Selena?"

"She hasn't regained consciousness yet, she's in critical condition at Porter Hospital. They're still look-ing for Ray Calhoun and they know he's driving a dif-ferent car now."

"Did they find out any more about him?" Isabel asked.

"They contacted MMI but there was no record of a Ray Calhoun, but he probably used another name."

Tony turned to Isabel. "If you're ready I can take you to a hotel now."

Isabel exchanged glances with Alex. "Actually I think I'd feel better staying here." Isabel noticed Tony's raised eyebrow. "If he found Selena at a hotel maybe he's looking for me at one, too. This is probably my safest choice right now."

"Makes sense to me, Isabel. I'll call you later, okay?" Tony pecked her on the cheek and saw himself out.

Isabel's eyes slowly came to rest on Alex. "I hope that's okay with you?"

"You know it is." The corners of his mouth curved up ever so slightly.

+++

John Wyatt looked forward to spending the next few days in Colorado. The humidity in Austin was at an all time high and he remembered how great the weather was that summer he worked in Snow Creek.

He returned once last year with Alex to visit Ted Roberts. Ted had been a buddy of theirs from college and he helped Alex get his business set up there.

Leaning back in his chair, John surveyed his large corner office. A wall of windows provided a beautiful view of the river. Framed artwork hung on the walls, along with his credentials as a certified accountant. Fine leather chairs pulled up to his massive wood desk and a bookcase lined the back wall.

Over the years he'd begun to take it all for granted. The job, the money, the security. But yet, he could never rid himself of the guilt. He tried to make it up to Alex in a number of different ways. However hard he tried though, Alex never seemed to find the right girl to take her place. Of course Alex was always polite and amusing with the women he dated. But Alex's eyes spoke for themselves. They lacked the passion John remembered whenever Alex was with Isabel Medina.

John walked over to the large cherrywood credenza and retrieved a folder marked Miscellaneous. The two letters lay neatly folded inside. Copies he kept for himself. The reason never clear but he saved them nonetheless.

Slipping them into his briefcase, he locked the credenza and switched off the light. Howard McCormick's words drifted through his mind. 'You did the right thing, son'.

۞ ۞ ۞

Over lunch, Alex insisted they stay close to home, telling her he felt like a sitting duck in public. "I can work from my office anyway."

Isabel helped clear the dishes, the monotonous task evoking a calming sense of normalcy. "How are your parents?"

The question immediately roused a defensive response he'd erected since he'd left. His answer always the same. Fine. Instead he replied honestly. "I haven't seen them in nearly a year. My father and I had some words and haven't spoken ever since." Isabel gave no indication of shock. "You're not surprised?"

Isabel's thick lashes blinked back at him. "I don't know. You two didn't always see eye to eye. I remember he was somewhat overbearing."

"That's putting it mildly. A dictator is more like it. I guess it was inevitable. I talk to my mother once in awhile, and I know it's hard for her but I think after all these years she understands. I just don't know how she's put up with it."

"Sometimes people mistake security for love, and then are too afraid to give it up."

Alex pondered her statement. Was she referring to something else? The money? It didn't matter now. He blamed his father for that. He believed Isabel wouldn't have taken the money if his father hadn't tempted her. And right now he didn't think he needed to add to her distress by discussing it. As a matter of fact he rather liked being here with her, talking with her, watching her. It was almost as if they'd bridged the past, the twelve years fading away right in front of his eyes.

After excusing himself to do some work in his office, Alex stared at the paintings in his office. The months following that summer he defied those sudden impulses to trash the picture, some stray filament of hope always interrupting the urge. The only remaining memento of that summer and he'd never really let it go. And now maybe...no, he wouldn't let himself think any more about it. He would just welcome the opportunity he had to see her again.

Rearranging some papers on his desk he saw his answering machine's blinking light. John's voice played back. 'Plan on being in Denver tomorrow, staying at the Marriott downtown. I'll give you call.' John and he called each other at least once a month. Brief conversations, mostly about work, and mutual friends. Even though John still worked for his father, John knew about their rift and never broached the subject. Wouldn't John be surprised when he told him about Isabel?

Chapter Eighteen

Alex decided on a break after spending nearly two hours tackling his work pile. He emerged to find Isabel sitting outside on the brick patio.

"Hey, do you want a soda or anything?" Alex asked, peeking his head out the french doors. Isabel only shook her head, never turning to acknowledge his presence. Something pricked his conscience. Her erect shoulders a clue. Stepping onto the patio he spied some papers spread out on the table. "Isabel? Are you okay?"

Her gaze continued to stare straight ahead. "Twenty thousand dollars?"

Alex dropped down into the seat next to her. Red rimmed eyes slowly met his and then moved back in the direction of the papers before her. Alex followed and instantly noticed a letter with familiar handwriting. He reached for it.

Mrs. Medina:

The agreed upon amount of $20,000.00 is enclosed. You assured me this would be sufficient to *keep your granddaughter out of my son's life. Alex will come to understand this and I'm sure will abide by it. Please be aware he may defy my wishes at first and try to contact her, but he'll come to see this is the best for all.*

-Howard McCormick

Alex resisted the urge to reach out and take hold of her hand. "Isabel, the money doesn't matter any more. I know Tochita probably thought it was the right thing to do for both of you."

"You knew?" Isabel's incredulous tone aroused his defenses.

"No, not then. The falling out with my father was when I discovered what he had done. I don't blame you."

"Blame me for what? That twenty thousand dollars is still sitting in an account." Isabel grabbed a worn bank book from underneath the documents and tossed it at him. "I never needed your damn money. I put myself through college and earned my own way. You arrogant ass. I would have never agreed to your father's terms even if—" Isabel's voice wavered.

"Isabel, I just assumed," Alex got to his feet the second Isabel stood up.

"Assumed what? That all I wanted was your money? That I'd agree to your father's little scheme. Go to hell, Alex. I thought I knew you. I guess that old adage 'love is blind' holds true." Isabel grabbed the paperwork and turned to go.

Alex remained rooted to the spot. Blown away by the emotional attack he felt flowing through him. God, she hadn't known. An overwhelming surge of tenderness enveloped his heart. She hadn't betrayed him. Yet a small shred of uncertainty toiled in his mind. Why didn't she try to contact him?

۞ ۞ ۞

Isabel couldn't hide forever. *Just give it time*, he told himself. Night was falling as he parked his rental car in the covered parking lot. The green orderly uniform would be the perfect disguise. When news of her death wasn't splashed all over the evening news he suspected the worse. He needed to find out her condition before he planned the rest.

It only took him fifteen minutes to find the wing where Selena Olivas lay in intensive care. Ray marveled at how easy it was to fool hospital security and personnel. The official looking badge affixed to his shirt lent him access to the hospital's charts without raising any suspicions. His steps felt lighter now as glided to her room. Keeping his head bent while appearing to read a chart, Ray managed to avoid any direct eye contact. But a familiar voice at the end of the

corridor stopped him dead in his tracks. Isabel stood
outside a closed door talking with someone in plain
clothes. Ray immediately dashed into the closest doorway. What luck! The anticipation of seeing Isabel lifted his mood. Now he'd just wait. Destiny was theirs.

۞ ۞ ۞

The cab ride over seemed endlessly long. The
driver's unexpected talkative mood only agitated her
further. Alex practically forbade her to go and insisted
they discuss things, which only infuriated her further.

Amazing how all that anger she stored up after
that summer came back twofold. It proved his wealthy
background only clashed with the hard working princi-
ples she had to live by all her life. She had moved on
and wanted the past to stay where it belonged.
Forgotten.

Initially Isabel planned on going to a hotel but
half-way there changed her mind. She had to see
Selena. After directing the cab driver to Porter Hospital
she wondered if she was doing the right thing. Stop
worrying. Ray wouldn't chance being in public and she
knew for a fact that a policeman had been assigned to
guard Selena's room.

After begging Detective Winters for permission
he agreed to let her visit. Accepting her desire to be

there in case Selena regained consciousness. The nurse indicated Selena came to a couple of times but with no visible signs of coherency. Isabel heard the steady rhythm of machines hooked up to Selena's motionless body. She knew they removed a bullet near the spine after it entered the side of her neck and lodged there. Her injured hand bandaged as well from what they assumed to be due in part to a defensive measure when he shot her.

A step closer and Isabel could see the rise and fall of her chest. So many questions scrolled through her head. Who was she? What was her relation to Tochita? Isabel watched the nurse adjust the I.V. and then exit the room. Her natural response was to whisper, but over the din of medical equipment she doubted anyone could hear her.

"Selena? It's Isabel Medina." Touching her hand to Selena's arm she leaned closer. "Can you hear me, Selena?" No response. Isabel carefully positioned herself on the side of the bed. The doctors could offer no concrete answers yet. Not sure yet of the bullet's damage but they were hopeful she would survive.

Once again her mind drifted back to the quarrel with Alex. How could he deem her capable of taking his father's money and betray the love they shared together? A love she'd given to him, physically as well as psychologically. A love she'd never experienced since. A love resulting in...no, she didn't want his pity. Or his guilt. Isabel fought the urge to give in to the emotional upheaval developing internally. Fearing its river of pain too hard to endure this time around.

In only twenty-four hours a whirlwind had blown through her life. And now seeing Alex added another dimension to an already complicated situation. It was only a coincidence she reminded herself. Except Tochita's words intruded upon her reasoning. 'There are no coincidences or chance happenings. Only a sign of God's guiding hand.' *Stop it, Isabel.* She needed to concentrate on finding some answers. Her life depended on it.

Chapter Nineteen

Ray discarded the hospital garb, but donned a new disguise of glasses and a baseball cap. He made himself comfortable in the general lobby's waiting area, near the elevator doors. This way he could see anyone coming or going. Visiting hours on the patient floors were over but Isabel was still in there. He made sure there were no other ways for her to exit without him seeing her.

His leg bounced up and down, as he considered the possibility of Selena gaining consciousness. Ray knew they suspected him in the shooting but something else bothered him. He didn't want Isabel finding out he was the one to blame for her grandmother's death. The rest he could explain but he knew she'd never forgive him for that. He didn't think he could bear her hating him. If he could just get the chance to be with her alone, to explain and make her see that he never meant for all this to happen. That after meeting her he'd decided to quit this work. All for her. He could make her happy.

Give it time, he reminded himself. He'd get his

chance. Possessing the perseverance to see things through always resulted in a favorable outcome. This time would be no exception.

Ω Ω Ω

Isabel awoke to a sound she couldn't place right away. There it was again. A low groan escaped through Selena's dried lips. Isabel pulled herself out of the chair she'd dosed off in during the night. The nurse's visits and the guard's periodic checks kept her from falling into a deep sleep. Isabel inched closer and watched Selena's eyes blink open several times.

"Selena, can you hear me?" Isabel asked, peering down at Selena's glassy stare. At first no recognition but then Isabel noticed the shifting gaze. The eyes roamed around the room until finally resting on her. "You're in the hospital, Selena. You're going to be okay. Do you understand?" Selena nodded and Isabel knew she should summon the nurse but hesitated. Wanting to be alone with her for just a moment longer.

"Selena, I want to help you. But first tell me how you knew my grandmother Tochita? Isabel detected the movement of Selena's mouth but nothing came out. She bent down closer. "I know Ray killed her, but why?"

Selena's eyes closed and Isabel's spirit waned.

Would she ever know the truth? Once again she settled herself next to Selena. Her fatigue stretching to all parts of her body. Again she heard a groan. Selena's eyes were open and focused on her. "Selena?"

"Tochita—my father." Selena paused for a breath. "A disc—Ray wants."

"But how was my grandmother involved?" Isabel held her breath, afraid she'd miss Selena's whispered words.

"I mailed disc—Tochita. Ray found me. You are..."

The door swung open. The nurse and guard both entered. "Selena's awake," Isabel offered, recovering from the startling intrusion.

The nurse checked Selena's vital signs. "Miss Olivas, can you hear me?" Selena acknowledged her. "I'll be back with the doctor. Don't let her exert herself," she said, turning to Isabel.

The guard phoned in the report after the doctor indicated it would be okay to question Selena in the morning after she rested awhile longer.

Isabel realized they wanted her to leave as well. Selena needed rest now. Isabel nodded understanding and left the room.

Waiting for the elevator she went over Selena's fragmented speech and wondered at her reference to Tochita and Selena's father. There had to be more. It didn't make sense.

Hopefully she'd learn the rest tomorrow after the police questioned her. Stepping into the lobby she spotted some payphones nearby. A clock above the nurses station read three-thirty. She'd left a message at work for Tony earlier about going to a hotel but she'd better follow up or else he'd have the police out searching for her.

Chapter Twenty

Alex awoke to the sound of thunder. The loud crack bursting into his unpleasant dreams. The alarm clock displayed seven thirty. After starting a pot of coffee Alex jumped into the shower. The hot water spray soothed his rattled nerves. Doubts plagued his brain all night long, robbing him of any sleep. Was she safe? At a hotel?

How could he let this happen? Now he'd never forgive himself. Isabel's life was in danger and he'd been a fool. The fiery rage in her eyes when he accused her of taking his father's money burned a whole right through him. Once again he let the almighty dollar cloud his judgment. Forgetting the simple truth, not everyone was motivated by greed. Amazing how he'd forced the pieces to fit. Isabel's guilt that summer seemed indisputable since she took off without saying good-bye and never answered his letters.

Over the years he had rehearsed the scene over and over in his head. He imagined they'd meet, talk, and all his questions would be answered. It all seemed so simple. Unfortunately he hadn't been prepared for the onslaught of emotions blazing through his heart and memories of the anger and hurt culminating in that summer's bitter end.

Knowing his father's role in it all only made matters worse. If only he'd met his father head on from the beginning. Just maybe he could have prevented it all. But at twenty two he never imagined his father's obsession to control everything would destroy the one thing he'd never found since. The pure and honest relationship he shared with Isabel.

After his third cup of coffee he dialed Tony's number. The answering machine picked up there as well as at the restaurant. He tried the pager number and waited. Thirty minutes later he tried it again. Still no response. The agonizing wait stirred up the worst in his imagination.

The knock on his front door sent him flying across the room. Maybe...just maybe. He swung the door open. "John?"

John shook the rain from his umbrella and set it near the door. "Hi. I came straight from the airport. Figured you'd be home, with the weather and all. Maybe you can drop me off at my hotel later.

"Sure, uhm, come in, John. I..." Alex's taxed mind tried to process John's presence.

"Alex, is something wrong? Did I come at a bad

time?" John followed Alex into the kitchen.

"Want some coffee?" Alex poured a cup and handed it to John without waiting for an answer. "I don't even know where to begin. It's been a little crazy."

"I'm all ears."

Alex recounted the events of the last couple of days. Ted Robert's party, seeing Isabel, the lunatic named Ray Calhoun involved in Tochita Medina's death and his attempt to murder another woman.

"Alex, this sounds so insane. You could get yourself killed getting involved."

"I know it sounds crazy but right now I'm worried about Isabel and where she went. I'll blame myself if anything happens to her. Remember the money my father paid her, she never knew about it. I saw the shock on her face when she saw my dad's letter in her grandmother's papers. Tochita put it in an account and never touched it." Alex ran both hands against the side of his head. "My father's dirty little ploy far exceeded anything I could have imagined. I'm just sorry it took me so long to figure it out."

John's somber expression puzzled Alex. He gave no response but turned away and walked to his briefcase sitting on the floor. Alex watched him pull out an envelope and return to face him.

"I guess this is as good a time as any. I had

hoped to explain, but there really is no excuse for what I did. Just plain selfishness. Here," John handed him the envelope. "Maybe this can help clarify some things."

"I don't understand."

"Read the letter. The first one's a copy of your dad's letter, the other is one from Tochita Medina. A few months after that summer I tried to undo the mess I had a hand in but then it was too late."

Alex felt as if the air had been sucked out of him. "You knew?" John's silent nod answered. Alex unfolded Tochita Medina's letter and began to read. The letter lacked any formal salutations.

I intercepted your letter today to my grand-daughter. I'm sure Howard McCormick would find it distressing to learn of it as we had an agreement. Isabel has accepted things now and trying to change it would only bring more pain and sorrow to her life. I will not allow it. I've done whatever possible to protect her from the same pain her mother suffered and I will do it again, at any cost. Isabel never need know about the money until after my death as it is in an account awaiting her decision, to do with it whatever she wants. I accepted the money on principle, after knowing Alex's part in it all, he would never be worthy of my grand-daughter's love. The loss of their baby was a blessing in disguise. I know she'll earn her own way in life with-

out the trappings of the McCormick's money. Keep to your end of the agreement Mr. Wyatt and you'll have what you want and so will I.

-Tochita Medina

"Baby?!" Alex waved the letter in John's face. Lost what baby, John?" Alex exploded.

"She was carrying your baby. I'm sorry, Alex. Your dad offered to pay for my college and then promised me a job if I agreed to help him get rid of her. I took it and—"

"My God, when will the lies end?" Alex made a fist and then swung. The punch landing squarely on John's chin, knocking him to the floor. Alex came at him. John scrambled to get up and away from Alex's rampage. His arms raised to diffuse the forthcoming blow.

A perfectly timed call saved John's hide from the pent up rage rolled up in Alex's fist. Alex inhaled deeply before answering the call trying to disguise the hostility in his voice. "Hello?"

"Alex. Is Isabel there?"

"Tony, no. I've been trying to reach you." Alex's anxiety escalated.

"She called me from the hospital last night. After she left your place she went to see Selena. And then about three-thirty this morning she called and told me she was heading to the Hampton Inn. She never checked in."

Alex slammed his hand against the wall. "It's my fault. I should've never let her go."

"I'm heading to meet with Detective Winters now."

"I'll be there." Alex hung up the phone and turned to see John's face buried in his hands. Alex shook his head. "I've got to go."

"Alex, I want to help."

"Just leave, John. I don't want your help." Alex grabbed a windbreaker and left John staring after him.

Chapter Twenty-One

Ray stroked the inside part of her upper arm, the skin soft and warm. A moan escaped from her lips. The tranquilizer would be wearing off soon. After her defiance last night he wasn't taking any chances. With her wrists bound tightly to the parking brake and the vehicle's alarm set, he let himself doze off occasionally during the night.

Isabel resisted him at every turn. Even when he'd produced a gun to get her into his car, she wavered a moment before conceding. He loved the fire in her eyes, as well as the fear he saw there, too. She'd come around.

Ray spent most of the night hatching a plan. After retrieving his gear and papers he was set to proceed with the next phase. Convincing Isabel she needed him. He would take care of her, show her all the places he'd been, give her anything she wanted. There was nothing left for her here anyway.

Isabel once again stirred in the passenger's seat. Her head bobbed back and forth before her eyelids opened. Confusion appeared first and then panic. He watched as she tried to jerk her arms free. Snapping her head around, her eyes rotated back to him.

"You might have a little headache, babe. Sorry about the sedative but you gave me no choice."

"What do you want from me, Ray?" Isabel recoiled when he tried to smooth the hair off her face.

"It's simple, Isabel. I want you."

"You're crazy. What makes you think I'd go with you?"

"You don't have anything here. Your grand-mother's gone and I can take care of you."

"She's gone because of you," Isabel cried out.

"Is that what Selena told you? She lied just like your grandmother did all these years. Did Selena tell you who she was?" Ray watched as Isabel shook her head and turned away. "Selena Olivas, born to a Peter A. Vasquez."

"What?" Isabel's head snapped around.

"Your father, right? Known as Auggie to every-one including his daughter Selena who was born ten years after you. Lived outside Albuquerque until his death from alcoholism two years ago."

"Ray, if this is another one of your twisted lies I don't want to hear it."

"All true, I have it all here if you want to see," Ray said, pointing to a portfolio in the back seat.

"Selena mailed Tochita a computer disc she stole from a guy in New Mexico. It's worth a lot more than what she wanted but she was just out to swindle some money. She's an idiot and stupidly made a deal with these guys who play for real."

"So they hired you to kill her off."

"It's what I do, Isabel, but not any more. Not after I met you. You've changed all that. I've got money saved and we'll go away and I'll never go back to it."

"I'd rather die." Isabel's eyes bore right through him.

The loathing he saw there ignited a low growing rage inside. He resisted the surging fury compelling him to strike her. He blew out several puffs of air gaining his self-control. She needed some more convincing. *Just give it time*, he reminded himself

Alex parallel parked across from the police station. He rested his forehead against the steering wheel trying to assimilate the mass confusion going on in his head.

Deep in his heart he felt a pang he'd never experienced. A staggering sadness. No wonder she was so defensive. He now understood the depth of her anger.

Why had she kept it from him? How did she lose the baby? Their baby. What happened? So many unanswered questions tormented his thoughts. This latest bombshell only added to his mounting anxiety.

Entering the station Tony waved him over to a desk he sat in front of. "Alex, they still have no idea where she is. The nurse at the hospital said she left Selena's room about three-thirty but she was by herself. A cab company had a no show fare at the hospital about the same time."

"Tony, you've met this Ray. Would he hurt her?"

"I don't really know. He always seemed a little too captivated with her, put her on a pedestal and she ate it up. But considering she hadn't let any guy get too close in a long time, it was understandable. I don't know what to think."

Alex hung his head low. He silently prayed for her safety. "I should've made her stay."

"Alex, it's not your fault. She's stubborn and headstrong."

He nodded. That was one of the things he had loved about her.

Detective Winters joined them shortly thereafter. "Does a Peter Vasquez ring a bell, Tony?"

"Well, I think Vasquez was Isabel's father's name."

"He's also the father of Selena Olivas. Raised her after her mother died in New Mexico. We're pretty sure that's the connection to Tochita Medina. She never mentioned Selena?"

"No, Tochita told us Isabel's parents died in a car accident when she was six. No other family." Tony shook his head. "Selena's her sister?"

"Looks that way. It fits. Selena steals this disc, needs a place to lie low, and comes up with Tochita Medina. Ray discovers the link and follows her here. Hopefully we'll find out more when she gives her statement. Unfortunately after Isabel talked with her she's never regained consciousness again. But the doctors are hopeful."

Alex pushed his chair back and jumped to his feet. "I can't sit around here and wait. We've got to find her."

Detective Winters assured them they were doing everything possible but with reluctance admitted he was at a loss as where to look next. They could be long gone by now.

The last statement didn't set well with Alex. "I don't think so." If she was at all able he knew Isabel would fight Ray every step of the way. And it was that shred of hope he held onto as he left the station. Tony and he decided to split up, exchanging cellular numbers to keep in touch. Tony headed in the direction of Snow

Creek and Alex would check out the hospital again and eventually make his way up to Snow Creek. They decided to meet back at Tony's restaurant by six.

Alex's visit to the hospital produced nil. The night shift had gone home and the guard on duty only confirmed what Detective Winters had told them. Alex scoured the parking lot on foot, practically checking each car's interior for a sign, any sign of Isabel. He combed area hotels, describing Isabel and Ray to the employees, but not a one remembered seeing them.

Alex tried to put together a scenario in his head. Ray could have easily taken off earlier, right after he shot Selena, but he didn't. It must be Isabel. What Tony said about him putting her on a pedestal, maybe he was so hung up on her he couldn't leave. And that might just be his undoing.

Chapter Twenty-Two

Even though the trunk of the car frightened her at first, she later realized she felt safer in there than under Ray's vigilant observation. The sedative left her feeling groggy and she'd dozed off several times. She held onto the fact that he would have killed her by now if he hadn't wanted something else.

Ray's story about Selena seemed far-fetched at first but now the pieces seemed to fit. The link connecting Tochita and Selena. Tochita's odd behavior began about the same time Selena started working for Tony, and Ray's arrival followed soon after. It all added up.

Isabel recalled the few times Tochita spoke of her father, always with a hint of resentment or contempt. Her last words 'she's evil like him'. Was she talking about Selena and her father? Why did Tochita lie to her? The lies about her family and Alex made her wonder how much more there was.

Tears slid over the bridge of her nose and out the corner of her eyes. She sniffed, trying to stop the flow.

With her wrists bound behind her she could hardly maneuver inside the small space. When would it all end? A tiny part of her brain wished she could just fall asleep and never wake up. The anguish of it all almost too agonizing to live with. Knowing the painstaking task of accepting the dishonesty of someone you love and trust incredibly hard to endure and live through. She'd done it once before, she didn't know if she could again.

The movement of the car seemed to slow and she could hear the crunching of gravel beneath the tires. Where the hell was he taking her? The question answered soon enough after he pulled her from the back and she recognized the stretch of dirt road near the Petersen's property. Ray had pulled the car off to the side, the shrubbery hiding it from view.

Isabel suspected it was after six as she noticed the twilight sky and its pink hues above them. Ray grabbed her bound wrists and directed her forward. The earlier downpour had stopped, leaving the ground beneath them saturated. Isabel slid in the mud as she tried to keep pace with Ray's persistent push from behind. He hadn't said a word yet and she had nothing to say. Somehow his face seemed different, distorted almost. The darkness under his eyes created a hollow-like appearance. His clenched jaw pulling the skin taut over his cheekbones. But it was the blank stare that frightened her. Sending a silent alarm to all corners of her mind. She couldn't shake its growing grip on her.

❦ ❦ ❦

By the time they reached the house, darkness had fallen. He kept the lights off. They could go undetected here for awhile, rest and cleanup. No one would suspect him to bring her here, and after he convinced her to pack some things for their little trip they'd be out of there before morning.

Ray untied her wrists. He watched as she rubbed them with her fingers. "Will you forgive me, babe?"

Isabel's head jerked around and her glaring stare answered his question.

"Come on, turn around," Ray said as he pulled his gun out. "We're doing a little packing. And I'm ready for anything, Isabel, so don't try anything foolish." He positioned the gun in the middle of her back and slid his other arm around her waist. She smelled so good. He felt her stiffen at his touch.

"I know you wanted me before, Isabel. I can make you want me again," Ray said, his voice low and raspy. His hand slid up the length of her waist and squeezed her breast. He felt her recoil back against him. Ray nudged his face into her hair and laughed. "Keep moving."

"I can't see anything Ray."

"It's your room, babe, and you know where everything is so get busy." He stayed close behind her as she pulled things out of drawers and then went to the closet. He slapped her hand away as she reached for the overhead light. "Let's skip the closet. I'll buy you whatever else you need." He didn't want to take the chance with her in the crowded closet space.

At the sight of her bed he recalled scenes of their lovemaking as vividly as if they just happened. He felt his ardor growing and an overwhelming desire to take her right now. He knew she'd resist so he'd have to use force, at least until she succumbed to his touch. Twisting her arm behind her back he placed the gun in the back of his trousers and pulled her back against him.

"Ray, you're hurting me."

He smoothed the hair off her neck. "I don't want to," he whispered in her ear. His lips kissed her warm and salty skin. Isabel tried wriggling free but he twisted the arm tighter. "Don't fight me, Isabel."

"Please, Ray, don't," she protested.

Ray's hand went to her breast again and she tried pushing it away with her free hand. "Stop, Isabel." He grabbed her shirt and pulled, buttons popped and material ripped as he exposed her skin to his fondling. A muffled whimpering sound came from Isabel's mouth.

Her body seemed more pliant against him. Maybe she was beginning to enjoy it.

🏆 🏆 🏆

Alex slightly heeded the highway's curving direction ignoring the occasional screech from his tires. He called Tony from a convenience store because his cell phone had lost its battery charge. He'd meet him at the restaurant. So far neither had any luck. Tony reported going to Isabel's place earlier and not finding anything to indicate they'd been there. He and his brother Joey had combed every place they could think of and still no trace of them.

Alex flipped on his headlights as he waited in the exit ramp with the rest of the commuters. Hard to believe Snow Creek had a traffic problem but it had grown considerably since he'd been there.

Once it got dark he feared the worst. They'd lose time and that scared him. Nighttime would be the perfect time to leave, or get rid of her. Alex forced the thought from his head. But something else occurred to him. Nightfall would be Ray's ally. And Isabel's place might give Ray the perfect spot to hide out. He may be reaching but it was worth a second shot.

He followed the frontage road out to where it forked and then down a familiar stretch of streets. More houses had sprung up and old buildings gone or replaced. There hadn't been much out here years ago and only one major intersection to turn at. Now it all looked so different. He looked for something he recognized and then saw the old grocery still standing and knew he'd gone too far. Turning around he realized he was near the entrance to the Petersen property. His headlights lit up a 'For Sale' sign but something else caught his eye. Another reflection behind it. Alex turned onto the dirt drive and almost missed it. A parked car sat nestled behind a hedge of wild lilacs.

Alex's heart beat wildly as he stepped around the car. The sticker in the window indicated it was a rental. He bent down to look more closely at the ground, his headlights illuminating muddy tracks heading away from the road. Turning off his headlights and parking his car, Alex grabbed a flashlight and followed the trail of footprints. The soft ground hindered his pace and he slipped twice before he reached the back side of the barn. His heart sank at the sight of the darkened house. Were they gone already? With flashlight in hand he made his way to the house, silently treading up the wooden steps. "Please be here," he whispered into the darkness.

Chapter Twenty-Three

Silent screams filled her head. This wasn't happening. Ray's crazed state frightened her. She knew she had to act fast. With her eyes adjusted to the darkness she saw the row of perfumes on her dresser table. Relaxing her body and ignoring his coarse hands, she carefully reached out, her fingertips touching the top of a tall slender bottle. She wrapped her hand around it and lifted it up slowly so as not to alert Ray's attention. She inhaled deeply and held it.

"That's more like it, Isabel," Ray's grating whisper sounded in her ear.

A thud came from the front room. They both froze instantly at the sound. But Isabel realized her chance and took her best shot, wielding the bottle over Ray. The glass smashed against the top of his head, the fragrance filling the air. Ray groaned and fell backward as Isabel escaped his clutches. Blindly running through the house she stopped paralyzed in her tracks. A flashlight roamed the interior of the living room. In back of her she heard Ray's groaning.

"Who's there?" Isabel's voice barely audible even to herself as her heart pounded in her ears.

"Isabel?" The flashlight moved towards her, its direct light blinding her momentarily. "Isabel!" Alex yelled as he rushed to her.

"We've got to get out of here."

Ray's footfall sounded behind them. Alex grabbed Isabel's hand and ran to the open front door, the window pane shattered as a bullet struck the glass. Together they bounded off the front porch.

"Over there," Isabel pointed to the garage studio doors. They secured the door by sliding the latch to secure it. Moonlight beamed in through the far window, illuminating very little of the interior. Isabel gladly received Alex's impetuous embrace. His strong arms a safe haven from Ray's repulsive molesting. The racing of his heart sounded in her ears.

"Are you okay?" Alex's low whisper brushed along side her face.

Isabel nodded against his chest. The incessant trembling of her body intensified at the noise of Ray's banging on the door.

"Open up, Isabel. I'm going to blow this fuck-ing door to pieces."

In one swift move Alex directed Isabel away from the door. He pushed her up the pull-down ladder heading to the loft overlooking the studio. "Stay up there."

"What are you going to do?" Fear gripped Isabel as she watched Alex push the ladder back up. Alex disappeared into the shadows. After several blows the latch gave. Isabel shrunk back into the shadows of the loft.

"Whoever the hell you are, you can't protect her from me. I'll kill her before I let you have her." Ray's ranting filled the confined space.

Isabel cringed at his words. In one instant the light went on and the gun went off. Straining to hear, Isabel edged herself closer to the edge. A shuffling sound ensued. She couldn't stand it any longer. She leaned over and saw the gun lying on the floor. Her eyes followed the noise to find Ray and Alex struggling with one another. Isabel grimaced at the sight of Ray slugging Alex in the face, knocking him backwards against her table of paints.

Without hesitating, Isabel climbed over the edge and dropped to the floor. She ignored the pain in her ankle. Scooping up the gun, it felt heavy in her trembling hands. "Ray! Stop!"

Caught unaware at the sound of Isabel's voice, Alex didn't see the shiny knife in Ray's hand, its blade stabbing his side. Alex's pinched face attested to the excruciating pain as he fell to the floor. Isabel screamed and pulled the trigger at the same time.

The bullet grazed Ray's thigh, ripping his pants. Blood oozed from the gaping gash. Bulging eyes stared back at her. "You missed." Ray's sardonic laugh enraged her further.

"Ray, stay back." Isabel desperately tried to hold the gun steady.

"What are you going to do now? Tie me up? Maybe the cowboy over here would like to watch." Ray's teeth flashed back at her like a wild animal.

Isabel looked over at Alex, his body sagged against the leg of a wooden table. What if...? No, she could see his chest rise and fall. "Move over there, Ray." Isabel motioned with the gun.

Ray ignored her demand. "Go ahead, Isabel. Pull the trigger. See what it feels like to wield that power. In an instant you can take someone's life." Ray snapped his fingers. "Like that."

"Is that what you felt when you killed Tochita?"

"I only wanted to scare her but the old bitch was stubborn. If she'd only told me where Selena was. God knows why she would protect her. She'd kept her a secret from you all these years."

The gun became increasingly heavy. Isabel saw the root of evil in Ray's eyes. The rationale between right and wrong had gone askew in his twisted brain. At that moment the pressure of the voices in her head threatened to do the same.

Ray took a step towards Isabel. "I took care of Selena. I had to finish my job. Like I told you, Isabel. It was just business. What you and I had together was real. Fate brought you to me."

A cold sweat chilled her skin. She shook her head. "No, Ray. Fate is for people meant to be together. Who want to be together. I don't want to be with you." Isabel took a step back. Ray's menacing scowl raised the hair on her neck. She gripped the gun handle tighter.

A moan from Alex distracted her concentration. Ray lunged. Isabel closed her eyes and squeezed the trigger. Ray took another step, hands clawing at the air. A thud sounded when he hit the floor. Isabel's hand dropped to her side still holding the gun. "Oh God help me."

"Isabel." Alex labored to sit up.

"Alex, don't move." Isabel fell to her knees beside him, depositing the gun on the table. She felt a sticky substance on her hand as she helped him to a sitting position. Blood stained her hands but she merely wiped them on her jeans. "I've got to call the police, Alex."

"Not yet. Don't go."

"Alex, you're losing blood." Isabel's voice quivered. Her mind vacillating between going for help or heeding Alex's wishes.

"Isabel, I thought I lost you. Did he hurt you?" Alex's eyes lowered to her exposed chest. She followed his gaze and understood his concern. Self-consciously she gathered the fabric together with her hand.

"No, I'm okay." Inadvertently she stroked his forehead, running her fingers through the thick hair curling at his hairline. Alex glanced up at her. The blue of his eyes bottomless in their depths.

"I'm sorry, Isabel." His face contorted in pain as he tried to move again. "I need to tell you something." Alex's strained voice frightened her but she let him continue. "I should have never doubted you."

"Alex, don't..."

"Please," he grimaced, "let me finish. I let my father interfere. I only saw what he wanted me to see. Why didn't you tell me about the baby?"

Isabel bit down on her lower lip to stem the influx of feelings flooding her heart. "Alex, this happened so long ago, we've moved on."

Alex interrupted. "I need to know, Isabel. I can't keep burying the past without answers."

"I was on my way to tell you. That day you waited for me, I was driving to see you, and then it happened. I saw the blood and lost control of my car. I miscarried. I called John from the hospital but you never came. I didn't know what to think." The tears flowed freely now. "And then no letters or calls, I—"

She turned away.

"You must have hated me." Alex gently traced his finger along the faded scar bordering her outer brow.

The sorrowful look covering his face moved her. The years of pent up anger crumbled, loosening its powerful command. As she viewed his face she noted the pale color and beads of sweat. "Alex, I'm going for help."

"I can move. Help me inside."

Isabel complied and helped him to his feet. Their pace slow as he leaned on her for support. After settling him on a chair Isabel raced to call the police. Next she pulled clean towels from her closet and went to Alex. "Here, let me put some pressure here." She watched his jaw tense but he remained silent. His eyes closed as he leaned back. Isabel prayed it wasn't **too** late.

۩ ۩ ۩

Sirens and flashing lights invaded the air. Isabel opened the door and directed the paramedics to Alex. Detective Shelton entered along with two other police officers. Isabel guided them back outside to the garage where Ray lay in a puddle of blood. Isabel drew back from the scene, the full impact of all that had transpired overpowered her senses. She fled back to the house and watched as they hoisted Alex into the ambulance.

"Wait! I want to go." Isabel crawled into the back of the vehicle and took a seat next to Alex's stretcher. An oxygen mask covered his mouth and she looked up to see one of the paramedics handing her a lightweight jacket. Her hand flew to the gaping opening of her shirt as she accepted his offering in silence.

Everything seemed to move at lightning speed once they reached the emergency room. They wheeled Alex off to surgery and a nurse accompanied Isabel to an exam room insisting she wait for a doctor to come and examine her. The act of holding it all together collapsed at the sight of Tony's face peeking into her room. The rush of despair came forth in heaving sobs. Tony cradled her in his arms, his voice soothing and reassuring. "It's all over, Isabel. You're safe now."

The doctor directed his instructions to Tony as if Isabel weren't capable of comprehending. "Her blood pressure's low and her vital signs are depressed. She's in shock. Lots of rest and a follow-up appointment with her doctor would be a good idea."

Tony thanked the doctor and turned to Isabel. "I'm taking you to mamá's. She insisted you come."

Isabel didn't argue. The thought of returning home didn't set well with her anyway. She wasn't ready to deal with all that had happened there. "What about Alex? Is he going to be okay?"

"Let me check, I'll be right back." Tony returned several minutes later. "He's still in surgery but the nurse said the doctors are optimistic about the outcome. Let's get going. We'll call in the morning and find out how he's doing."

As they drove, Isabel tried to fill in the blanks for Tony. His endless list of questions depleting any residual energy she had left. Finally she asked if it couldn't wait until morning. Tony had no objections and apologized for grilling her.

Once they reached the Perez home, *tía* Anita's doting manner eased Isabel's objection to being taken care of. Tucked into bed like a child, Isabel attempted to give in to her fatigued state yet she could not extract the images of her ordeal from her head. Ray's face taunted her, his rough hands, the gun, the blood, she squeezed her eyes shut. Only one positive image emerged. Affectionate blue eyes holding her spellbound. "Alex," she whispered, succumbing to her body's weariness.

Chapter Twenty-Four

An elderly man in a wheel chair persisted in striking up a conversation with Alex. The man maneuvered himself near where Alex leaned up against a ledge just outside the hospital's entrance doors.

"You waiting for a ride?" The man's frail body belied the boisterousness of his voice. A strong southern accent caught Alex's attention immediately.

"Yes sir." Alex replied checking his watch. Tony should arrive any minute now. He had planned on taking a taxi over to Isabel's but Tony wouldn't hear of it.

"All except for that bruise on your face, you look like a healthy young man."

Without going into details, Alex nodded. "Clean bill of health. Worst part was the hospital stay, if you know what I mean?"

"Sure do. Been here off and on for the last year, but if I had it my way I'd never come back. But I do it for the wife. She thinks all these doctors can help me and it makes her feel like she's doing something.

Nothing worse than feeling helpless watching a person die."

Taken back by the man's frankness, Alex remained silent, yet his face must have conveyed his dismay.

"Nothing to be feared in dying, son. It's only the things you do while living you should worry about. I look back now and the things that made my life good were the things right smack there in front of my face. The best thing was finding my Irene. Almost let that woman slip through my hands. I was a stubborn fool and almost missed spending close to fifty years with a woman I could never ever replace."

Alex nodded his head as he listened to the man who obviously had some things to get off his chest and chose Alex as his confidant.

The old man continued. "If you ever find your true love, mark my words you'll know it by the way you feel when you look into her eyes. My Irene, her fading gray eyes still speak to me. It's like I can see all the years of love mirrored there. Remember this, son. A lifetime is not long enough to let any chance at love slip away. Take it from an old man who's near the end, the only thing I can take with me is the love in my heart. Nothing else really matters."

Alex looked up to see Tony's car pull into the circular drive leading to the entrance. A chest racking cough seized the man. "Sir, is there someone I can get for you?"

"I'm okay. It comes and goes." His brittle fingers clasped a wadded up tissue he used the dab the corners of his mouth.

"My ride's here now. You're sure you're okay?" Alex asked moving closer to the curb waving at Tony.

"Don't worry yourself none. You've been more than kind listening to my prattling on."

Alex shook the man's extended hand. "It was my pleasure, sir." He stepped off the curb, waiting for Tony to get around a car unloading.

Hopping in the car, Alex looked over to see a large silver-haired woman bent over the old man. He received the man's wry smile as he waved good-bye.

"Tony, I appreciate the ride."

"No problem, I retrieved your car from the Petersen's and parked it at Isabel's. You doing okay?"

"Just a little sore is all. Rest and nothing strenuous, doctor's orders." Alex sighed. "I'm just glad to be going home."

"Saving damsels in distress is a dangerous hobby."

Alex laughed at Tony's humorous appraisal of 'rescuing' Isabel. "I think if you asked Isabel it was the other way around. Besides, Isabel has never needed anyone to rescue her."

"At least she wouldn't willingly admit to it," Tony countered.

"Is she doing okay?"

"Yeah, she's at my mom's, whose constant vigilance will probably send Isabel home sooner than intended. It'll take awhile to recover from all this but she's tough." Tony paused. "You know, Isabel is like a little sister to me. And this may be none of my business, but I think you two owe it to yourselves to iron out your problems. I know it happened a long time ago but I don't think she ever got over you. Even though she'd like everyone to believe she did."

"I don't know, Tony." Alex rolled down his window, suddenly feeling a little warm.

"I think you both deserve to know the truth."

Alex changed the subject when he spotted the 'For sale' sign. "Is that the Petersen property?"

"Good memory. Old man Petersen died a few months back and Mrs. Petersen finally decided to sell it. None of the kids wanted it."

"I remember Isabel wanting to buy that piece if they ever sold."

"Sure, but she doesn't have that kind of money. The house needs some work but the stables and land are still in pretty good shape. It'll have to be a special buyer. Snow Creek doesn't have all that much to offer in terms of jobs so it'll have to be someone who's independently wealthy or doesn't mind a commute."

Alex recalled the stream running through it and the rolling meadows where he and Isabel spent hours talking about their hopes and dreams. For an instant it seemed like yesterday. He had to shake his head to remind himself that it was another place and time.

"Here we are." Tony pulled up along side Alex's car. Yellow police ribbon draped across the garage doors. "I'm going to stay and pick this stuff up. Somebody is supposed to come by later and clean up the rest. I don't want Isabel to return to all these reminders."

Alex slipped his key ring on his finger and swung the keys around it in a circular motion. "I think I'll head home. Thanks for everything, Tony."

"Sure. One question. This Ted Roberts, he's a good guy, right?"

Alex smiled. "One of the best, Tony. You won't go wrong with him." Alex slid into the driver's seat, rolling down the windows on both sides. "Tony, if you need anything, look me up."

"You do the same." Tony waved back as he ripped down the yellow tape.

Alex drove slowly along the dirt road, stopping for a minute in front of the 'For Sale' sign. It sure was a great piece of land he thought to himself. Someday he'd like to have some property like this, great for his business, some horses, and well, a family, too. Wishful thinking right now. He had other things to worry about. Like making sure the client he was supposed to meet yesterday would accept his apology for not showing up or calling. He just hoped he didn't have to go into details. The story seemed a little far-fetched even to himself.

☙ ☙ ☙

A slight breeze stirred the leaves of the nearby rose bushes. Isabel settled herself into one of the back porch wicker chairs with a tall glass of ice tea nestled in her hand. Detectives Shelton and Winter's visit this morning left her feeling drained. She played out the scenario three or four times before they were satisfied. They reported on Selena's condition. So far she had cooperated with them and after her release from the hospital next week they would begin criminal proceedings.

It left Isabel feeling somewhat troubled. How was she suppose to feel about all this? A sister she never knew who from the very beginning showed an unexplainable animosity towards her. Shouldn't she feel something? After all, they were blood related. It was all so tiresome.

For the past week she'd kept herself occupied with chores around the house. Tackling closets and cupboards, she disposed of accumulated junk and splashed a new coat of yellow paint on the kitchen walls. Tony and tía Anita helped her back into the studio, the first steps difficult but necessary to come to terms with it all. After a few days she stopped seeing Ray's grim face at every turn. Tony stayed the first two nights, then Joey, but she put an end to it after realizing how easy it would be to keep accepting their presence.

The best distraction had been the phone call. A gallery owner in Denver wanted to see her about doing an exhibit. The woman had seen her work at Tony's restaurant and loved her paintings, buying two for herself. Ecstatic described her mood for hours afterward. Finally a step towards her dreams.

Gazing out into the overgrown backyard she turned to see Tony's car coming up the drive. Her puzzled expression remained as she greeted him. "What are you doing here?"

"I got kicked out of my office for the afternoon. The police are there downloading some information off my computer. I guess Selena used it as a safekeeping measure."

"They didn't mention it earlier." Isabel noticed the box Tony carried up the steps.

"I think they're trying to keep this as quiet as possible. The information Selena stole is highly confidential and I think the police are trying to put a case together against MMI. Selena told them MMI was involved in hiring Ray to go after her. I guess she didn't realize she'd made a deal with the people she stole it from in the first place." Tony followed her inside. "Alex was at Ted's office and gave me this to give to you."

"Thanks. I haven't started on Tochita's room yet."

"Give yourself time, Isabel. You might ask mamá to help you."

"I'll think about it." Isabel walked to the refrigerator. "Want some ice tea?" Tony nodded and she poured him a glass. Her eyes fell on the box. "You know, Tony, I can't believe Tochita lied to me all this time. I thought she was supposed to love me."

"Isabel. You know she did. She must have felt she needed to protect you. Mamá always said she blamed herself for your mother's death. Maybe Tochita thought she'd lose you like she did your mother." Tony placed a hand on her shoulder. "Without a doubt, Isabel, Tochita loved you more than anything else. You have to remember that."

"It's just so hard right now. This whole time I blamed Alex for what happened. Tochita knew how much I cared for him yet she took the money to keep us apart. I just don't understand what she thought she was accomplishing by ruining something that should have

M. Louise Quezada

been my choice."

"But think about it, Isabel. The money is still sitting in the account. She must have had second thoughts or else it would be gone."

"Well, I'm giving it back. I need to start with a clean slate before I can move on."

"Who are you trying to convince, me or yourself?"

Isabel's sidelong glance revealed he'd touched a nerve.

"Okay, I'll leave it be. I'm going to lunch with my new *chica*. I'll call you later."

Tony's words reminded her of the conversation *tía* Anita tried to have with her the other night. 'He was your first love *mi hita*. He'll always have a special place in your heart. Sometimes before you can move forward, you have to take a step back. You and Alex may have been too young but it seems others played a big part in keeping you from one another. Don't fool yourself into thinking that you can just forget it all. The heart remembers. You can see with all that has happened the past eventually catches up.'

Isabel's finger traced around the rim of her glass. So many unanswered questions. The lies and secrets. Tochita's death. Selena and Ray. And trying to deal with the fact she pulled the trigger that killed Ray. She scarcely remembered those seconds when she fired the gun. Detective Shelton reassured her what she was experiencing was normal. He recommended a police psychologist to help her adjust to the trauma she'd been through. To think what might have happened had Ray...

Isabel forced the tormenting images aside. Something consoling tugged at her thoughts. Even though she'd succumbed to Ray's sexual advances, a victim of her own grief, she never let him in. Never let him touch that part of her which she buried a long time ago with her feelings for Alex. The part of her heart that loved without reservation. The bold strength of a love that knows no boundaries. Maybe her instincts had been there and she'd only refused to listen to them. She had to believe this.

Chapter Twenty-Five

Not a cloud in the sky. The past week brought a round of continuous thunderstorms but today no sign of rain yet. Determined to keep herself busy, Isabel spent most of her days in the studio. An exhibit planned for after the first of the year spurred her on. School would begin in a couple of weeks and Isabel looked forward to a routine again.

Yesterday she had finished going through Tochita's personal things. The box Tony returned sat unopened until this morning. Everything was there except the bracelet. She wondered. Did he keep it? Half a dozen times she thought about calling Alex but in the end always talked herself out of it. She felt indebted to him, he did almost die because of her, but it didn't change anything.

Tony's call earlier about the Petersen property disappointed her. Before mailing Alex the check last week she debated about using it to put down on the Petersen's property. But then reality hit, she'd never be able to make those kind of payments anyway. Besides she couldn't keep the money. It only reminded her of the past.

Emotions swam close to the surface and she tired of trying to figure it all out. A walk before going back into the studio would help clear her head. When she reached the stream, the banks swelled higher than usual due to the recent rain. Isabel removed her sandals and waded through the cold water. She followed it downstream for several feet before hopping to the other side. With her interest piqued, she decided to pay a visit to the Petersen house. Maybe the new owners would be there.

Isabel kept to the meadow's soft grass, avoiding the muddy dirt drive. Humming a tune to herself she gazed appreciatively at her surroundings. The recent rainfall greened up the grounds, and flowers bloomed wildly. A picturesque scene to relish.

Nearing the house Isabel looked up for signs of inhabitants. She stopped dead in her tracks. A silver blue blazer sat parked in the opened garage. Isabel's head reeled with confusion. No, it can't be. Her breath came in shallow spurts as her eyes skimmed along the perimeter of the house. Turning to go, a high pitched yapping sound deterred her escape. A golden haired puppy came bounding down the drive. Immediately forgetting her reason for leaving, she bent down to rub the puppy's tummy.

"You're a friendly fella." Isabel picked him up and giggled as the puppy licked her face. Temporarily engrossed in her new found friend Isabel didn't hear anyone approaching.

"I see you've met Eddie."

Isabel's laughing eyes turned to his. "One of Liza's?"

Alex nodded and tucked his hands into his back pocket. Clad in a red T-shirt, Alex looked fully recovered. The tips of his black cowboy boots peeked out from under the hem of his jeans.

His stance reminded Isabel of a shy boy meeting a girl for the first time. For some reason she felt the need to put him at ease. "I didn't mean to intrude. Are you my new neighbor?"

"Yes. I just moved in yesterday. I debated calling you but my mind was made up and I figured you'd just have to get used to it." The curve of his lips hinted at a grin.

"I see. You have that right. Your injuries seemed to have healed."

"Pretty much. I get a little sore if I over do it. And you?"

"I'm good." Alex's intense stare made her feel uncomfortable.

"I have some ice tea in the fridge."

"I really should get going." Isabel's hand gestured back to her place.

"Please. I'd like to talk." Alex beckoned.

"Besides, I think Eddie's taken a liking to you."

Isabel smiled. *Now or never,* she thought. She walked to the stairs and took a seat on the top step, watching Eddie wrestle with a stick in the dirt.

Alex joined her with two ice cold glasses in hand. He cleared his throat before speaking. "I know you must be going through some difficult times right now, Isabel. And this may not be the best time to bring this up but I've spent the last twelve years shoving my feelings deep down inside and after this past week I realize I need to deal with them head on. We have to talk about it." Alex turned so he could face her directly.

Isabel avoided his eyes. Her first reaction had been to run, avoid the conflict, and just leave it be, but in her heart she knew he was right. Time may have mended the wounds, but without answers and forgiveness they never completely healed.

Alex began, lacing his fingers around his glass. "I keep thinking back to that day I left. After waiting for you all night I came by here early in the morning. Tochita came to the door and when she told me you'd left with Michael and Joey I had no reason to doubt her. She acted odd but I couldn't put my finger on it. Obviously my father had already gotten to her. I know it doesn't do any good but I keep wondering what if I had stayed, what if—"

"Alex, you're right, it doesn't do any good, we can't change what happened."

"I only wish I had tried harder. To think of what you went through. Losing the baby, our baby. I can understand you hating me."

Isabel swallowed hard, touched at his genuine concern. The years of anger melted away the walls she'd constructed to keep the anguish at bay. At a loss for words, she only nodded. They both watched as Eddie fetched the stick Alex tossed into the grass.

"I know that thank you isn't enough, but I do appreciate all you did for me. You nearly died trying to help me and I'll never forget it." Isabel's eyes remained on Eddie.

An uneasy moment of silence passed before Alex spoke. "I'd do it again."

Her breath caught in her throat as a warm sensation spread across her skin. She recognized the affection in his voice. But she fought the steamrolling sentiment rising from somewhere deep down, afraid of the heedless effect on her heart.

"I know you're having a hard time with what Tochita did. And this may be hard to believe but I don't blame her. My father is very persuasive and manipulative and will stop at nothing to get what he wants. It took me a long time to figure that out. I'm sure the money was too great a temptation. And Tochita already had misgivings about me and my family."

"But it still doesn't make it right." Isabel glanced down to see Alex's hand upon her arm. She hadn't notice the gesture.

Alex leaned in closer. "I know Tochita loved you more than anything, Isabel. I don't think she ever meant to hurt you or cause you any pain. I'm sure my father's bribe and the shock of you being pregnant frightened her."

"It's just so hard to understand, Alex. I know she's gone, but how can I ever forgive her? She lied about you and Selena. What other lies and secrets don't I know about?"

Alex reached behind him and pulled a folded note from his back pocket. "Maybe this will help. John Wyatt brought me this letter. I guess he couldn't live with the guilt any longer. I was so angry I nearly beat the hell out of him."

Isabel unfolded the letter. The quiver in her bottom lip warned of the tears she fought back. A useless attempt. One by one, each tear drop spilled down her cheek.

"What she did was wrong, Isabel, but in her eyes she was doing it for you," Alex assured her. "You have to believe that."

Rising from the step, Isabel rested her back upon the railing. She teetered back and forth between anger and sorrow. Anger at Tochita's actions and sorrow from the love Tochita evidently felt justified her decision. Staring overhead she noted the dark clouds forming. Another rainstorm. Her gaze returned to Alex. In his clenched hand the silver bracelet dangled. When he glanced up he must have seen the confusion on her face.

"I know this belongs to you." Alex started. "At first I didn't know why I kept it. A memento, a souvenir, another reminder of what I loved about that summer." He stood to face her. "You know, Isabel, when I saw you at Ted's, it was like time stood still. Like my heart remembered exactly how I felt back then. As if it had only skipped a beat and picked up right where it left off."

Isabel shook her head as she felt Alex press the bracelet into her palm, enclosing his hands about hers. "I don't want this. I don't need a reminder." Alex's voice vibrated with emotion. "I want you."

It was as if his words were the key to a part of her heart she'd kept locked away. The dam burst, sending forth a swell of emotions she'd thought were long gone. Without a word, Isabel flew down the steps into the rain already falling. Ignoring little Eddie's barking she kept on going. Down the drive, her feet sliding in the mud. Alex's voice calling out behind her.

"Isabel. Stop!" The deafening sound of thunder rumbled through the sky. "Isabel!" he yelled again.

The clouds above opened, heavy rain poured down. Isabel didn't care. At the stream she stopped, looking for a place to cross. A second later Alex grabbed her from behind. She squirmed in his arms, trying to free herself. "Alex, let me go."

"Not this time, Isabel." He pulled her close against him, trapping her arms at her sides. "I didn't mean to scare you off. But you can't leave yet, not until we finish this."

Tears mingled with the rain drops on her face. Isabel turned herself around in his arms. She cried into his chest, allowing herself to be held and comforted by his strong arms.

When the sobs ceased, Alex gently tilted her head up. "There's never been anyone since you, Isabel. I could never find what we had with any other person. God, I tried, thinking I could rid you from my head, but it never worked. Your face, your eyes, your smile. Always there etched in my mind."

Water dripped off the ends of his hair onto his face. Isabel reached up and smoothed the thick curls back. "Alex, can we ever repair the damage?"

"I know you feel betrayed and lied to, but that's all behind us now, Isabel. I'm here with you. You can always trust me." His eyes beckoned with a gleaming intensity, awakening in her a forgotten passion that took hold of her instantly.

Being locked in his embrace seemed so natural and familiar. The perfect fit. Isabel stared at his mouth. Their soaked clothes molding them together.

"Can I kiss you, Isabel?"

Without hesitating, she nodded. The question stimulating the memory of their first kiss.

His mouth lowered to hers. The warmth of his lips seemed to spread down her entire being. She sensed her body's craving. All reasoning lost to the glowing passion encompassing her soul.

Alex pulled away first. "Once again, Isabel Medina, you take my breath away."

A warm flush rose to her cheeks. She smiled, catching her lower lip between her teeth. "You know, your eyes still hold me spellbound."

Alex's mouth curled upward at the corners. "I told you. You were the first and last one I'd cast a spell on."

"I guess it's still working." Eddie barked at their feet. "Is Eddie named after anyone in particular or you just thought it was cute?"

Her teasing brought a curious grin to Alex's face. "If you must know, I met this man at the hospital, actually he kind of cornered me. Started rambling on about love, and his wife, and how I'd know my true love by seeing the love mirrored in her eyes. Well, it took a couple of days before the words sank in and then I saw a picture in the newspaper resembling him. He had died the next day. His name was Eddie Kane and I guess at one time he was a famous songwriter."

"Okay. So you named your dog after a dead songwriter?"

Alex's gaze held hers. "I named him for us. Because I know what Eddie meant. It's the way I feel when I look into your eyes, Isabel. I know you feel it too. We've always had a connection drawing us together. I don't want to go through life not loving you."

Isabel could almost feel her heart free itself of its bindings. The rigid restraints that held all her emotions in check ripped away by his words. She wrapped her arms behind his neck, pulling him close. Her lips brushed against his, lightly at first. Teasing and playful. Alex's hands gently cupped her face, his impassioned eyes pulling her into their depths. Their kisses deepened with a growing urgency. Responding to her desire, he lifted her up into his arms, carrying her back to the house. Up the drive and around to the back door, water dripping from their drenched bodies.

He placed Isabel back on her feet and closed the door after Eddie made his way back in. The boyish grin on Alex's face made her heart sing. Everything felt so absolutely right.

Their kissing resumed and within minutes they'd stripped each other of their soaked clothing. Wet footprints stamped on the wood floor as they crossed over the gate corralling Eddie from the rest of the house. Alex took her hand and guided her through the maze of boxes into his room. The white linens she remembered from his house lay exposed on the unmade bed. Alex turned and pulled her close against him. "I love you, Isabel. But I want you to be sure."

Isabel's finger's gently brushed his lips. "Shh. You can't possibly think I'd say no now. I love you, Alex. And now I realize I never stopped loving you."

The coolness of the sheets went unnoticed as their bodies fell upon the bed. His fingers gently caressed the base of her throat and trailed down the middle of her body, his lips eventually following its path. As his mouth grazed her nipples she found the fiery response intoxicating. Wanting to share her body's passion, she returned his caresses. Her fingers traced along his damp body and the hard muscles of his backside. Alex rolled onto his back with her wrapped in his embrace. Straddling his waist she pushed up and began her pathway of light and teasing kisses. His groans of pleasure filling her ears. Alex pushed himself to a sitting position, once again devouring her lips. Both hungry as their hands and eyes explored one another. Their shared intimacy hypnotic and liberating.

Every nerve ending was on fire and Isabel could no longer stand it. "Take me, Alex," she urged.

Alex searched her face. "You're more beautiful than I remembered," he whispered before lifting her up to receive her.

Their bodies moved as one. Passion ignited. She climaxed seconds before he did, aware of his struggle to hold back until he knew she was satisfied. This was making love, she thought.

Lying back against the pillows, Alex gathered her in his arms as she positioned herself along side him. Isabel raised herself off his chest. In his eyes she saw the true depth of their love. Maybe Eddie was right.

Through heavy lids he smiled back at her. His thumb traced the scar along her brow. A brief frown wrinkled his forehead. "I'll always be here for you, Isabel. No matter what, don't ever doubt that."

Isabel bent and kissed him long and deeply before answering. "I won't, Alex. I promise." Finally she understood what her heart always knew.

The End

Genesis Press titles are distributed to the trade by
Consortium Book Sales & Distribution, Inc.
1045 Westgate Drive
St. Paul, MN 55114
1-800-283-3572 phone
612-221-0124 fax

Genesis Press

315 3rd Avenue North
Columbus, MS 39701
Tel: (601) 329-9927
Fax: (601) 329-9399
http://www.colom.com/genesis

Mail Order Form to:
Genesis Press, Inc.
Order Department
P. O. Box 388
Ashland, OH 44805
Or Call 1-888-INDIGO-1

Bill to:
Name _____
Address _____
City _____ State ____ Zip ____
Phone _____
Ship to: (if different from above)
Name _____
Address _____
City _____ State ____ Zip ____
Phone _____

SBN #	TITLE	TYPE	PRICE	QTY	PRICE EACH	TOTAL
-885478-65-8	Passion's Blood	HC	$22.95			
INDIGO						
-885478-24-0	Gentle Yearning	PB	$10.95			
-885478-27-5	Midnight Peril	PB	$10.95			
-885478-29-1	Quiet Storm	PB	$10.95			
-885478-33-X	No Regrets	HC	$15.95			
-885478-32-1	Naked Soul	HC	$15.95			
-885478-47-X	Dark Embrace	PB	$4.99			
-885478-34-8	Pride and Joi	HC	$15.95			
-885478-35-6	A Love to Cherish	HC	$15.95			
-885478-41-0	Rooms of the Heart	PB	$4.99			
-885478-37-2	Indiscretions	PB	$4.95			
-885478-54-2	Truly Inseparable	HC	$15.95			
INDIGO 2						
-885478-38-0	Hearts Remember	HC	$15.95			
-885478-50-X	Forbidden Quest	PB	$10.95			
KID GENESIS						
-885478-43-7	What's Under Benjamin's Bed	PB	$8.95			
-885478-45-3	Dreamtective	PB	$4.50			
-885478-42-9	Brent Dad 1: Baseball	PB	$3.50			
-885478-44-5	To Be Me...Or Not To Be Me	PB	$8.95			
FICTION						
-885478-25-9	Montgomery's Children	PB	$14.95			
-885478-28-3	The Honey Dipper's Legacy	PB	$14.95			
-885478-49-6	Secret Library, Vol. 1	PB	$18.95			
-885478-39-9	Next to Last Chance	HC	$24.95			
-885478-55-0	The Joker's Love Tune	HC	$24.95			
-885478-16-X	Hidden Memories	PB	$10.95			
-885478-48-8	Go Gentle Into That Good Night	HC	$12.95			
-885478-40-2	Making Travel Count: A Guide To Educating & Entertaining Your Children On The Road	TPB	$15.95			
-885478-46-1	How to Write Romance For The New Market & Get Published	PB	$16.95			
-885478-31-3	Uncommon Prayer	PB	$9.95			
-885478-22-4	The Smoking Life	HC	$29.95			
-885478-30-5	Lasting Valor	HC	$24.95			
BACKLIST						
-885478-21-6	Passion	PB	$10.95			
-885478-29-1	Quiet Storm	PB	$10.95			
-885478-23-2	Again, My Love	PB	$10.95			
-885478-07-0	Breeze	PB	$10.95			
-885478-02-X	Everlastin' Love	PB	$10.95			
-885478-10-0	Love's Deceptions	PB	$10.95			
-885478-06-2	Whispers in the Sand	PB	$10.95			
-885478-09-7	Shades of Desire	PB	$8.95			
-885478-00-3	Careless Whispers	PB	$8.95			
-885478-05-4	Dark Storm Rising	PB	$10.95			
-885478-08-9	Love Unveiled	PB	$10.95			
-885478-15-1	Love Always	PB	$10.95			
-885478-13-5	Nowhere to Run	PB	$10.95			
-885478-17-8	Reckless Surrender	PB	$6.95			
-885478-12-7	Yesterday Is Gone	PB	$10.95			

Shipping and Handling fees are $3.00 for the
first book and $1.00 for each additional book.

Subtotal: _____
Shipping and Handling: _____
TOTAL: _____